BLIND DATE

Back in the Game

Kay Doherty

Dekker Callan is content with his life though he knows something is missing. Wanting the kind of love his friends share with their partners, Dekker is talked into taking part in a modeling and dating show as part of a fundraiser. He immediately falls in love with the anonymous, sexy voice on the other side of the wall, but fate has a surprise in store—his mystery man isn't single.

Slade Gannon wasn't supposed to take part in the dating show. That spot was for his roommate, Phil, who becomes ill and asks Slade to take his place. Slade has just recently gone through a breakup with his cheating boyfriend, George. Shocked and pleased when he wins the interest of handsome Dekker Callan, before he can go on the obligatory blind date, his ex asks for a second chance. Believing Dekker can't possibly be as good on the inside as he looks on the outside, Slade agrees.

Dekker and Slade hit it off immediately, drawn to each other despite Slade being involved with someone else. They finally get their opportunity to be together when Slade finds out his boyfriend is still cheating, but just as they seem to discover the happiness they've been waiting for, George throws them one last hurdle—and this one may prove to be insurmountable.

This is a work of fiction. All characters, places and events are from the author's imagination and should not be confused with fact. Any resemblance to persons, living or dead, events or places is purely coincidental.

Published by
NineStar Press
PO Box 91792
Albuquerque, New Mexico, 87199
www.ninestarpress.com

Warning: This book contains sexually explicit content which is only suitable for mature readers.

Print ISBN # 978-1-911153-90-0
Print Cover by Natasha Snow
Edited by B.J. Toth

Dedication

For Grandma Mary Doherty who encouraged me to write
and Mama Peggy Clason for insisting I finish.

Acknowledgements

Ever since I can remember, I've been telling people that I want to be published. After meeting my husband, every time those words passed my lips, his reply was, "Better get writing, then." Thank you, Michael, for being a loving, supportive nag.

I'd like to thank my father, Mike Doherty, who put a pen and paper in my hand and an idea in my head that ultimately turned out to be the best therapy ever known. To my mom, Pat Doherty, who constantly read what I wrote and insisted that I was a good writer and would one day see my dream come true.

Thank you to NineStar Press and my editor, BJ, for giving me this incredible opportunity and guiding me through every little step of the process.

Thank you to Professor Laurence Washington, who taught me how to be a better writer despite my never having set foot in his classroom. The guidance was appreciated and will not be forgotten.

To every single person who has ever set foot in my life and made an impact, positive or negative, thank you. You're probably in one of my novels.

Chapter One

"Hell, no," Dekker said a little too loudly. His friend Alek shushed him as several heads in the restaurant turned at his raised voice. Dekker leaned across the table and repeated more quietly, "No, no, and no. I'm not doing it."

"It's for charity," Alek said for the tenth time.

"And whose brilliant idea was that, huh? What guy in his right mind would willingly do that to himself?"

"Hey, it was my idea," Alek said defensively. "We have to do something to bring money into the clinic. I'm open to other options if you've got any."

Dekker leaned back in the booth with a silent huff. He hadn't meant to insult his friend, but the last thing he wanted to do on a Saturday night was take part in a beauty contest/dating show. What Alek was doing was noble. Dekker wouldn't deny that. HIV was a disease that needed to be eradicated. The Cleo Farnes Clinic, where Alek worked as finance director and spearheaded fundraising events, serviced those already infected. HIV wasn't just a gay man's disease, and the clinic treated all men, women, and children, but Alek's idea for this fundraiser was solely directed at gay men. The clinic was largely dependent on federal funds that always fell short and a whole lot of volunteer hours. Providing low-cost and sometimes-free care wasn't free for those offering the help. They had bills. Some had salaries. Supplies and medications cost money. Money the clinic was very much in need of, but this?

"Would it really kill you to just sit in a chair without a shirt on and answer a few questions? Who knows? You might actually meet someone. Did you think of that?" Alek asked.

Dekker lowered his eyebrows. Alek was becoming desperate. The man was close to begging now. Dekker blew out a breath and crossed his arms over his chest.

"Fine. I'll do the dating game, but I'm not doing that catwalk thing," he said.

Alek's face instantly changed. He became more animated, relieved that Dekker had finally caved. It would seem Dekker's agreement to the dating portion of his fundraiser wasn't enough for him, however.

"The modeling show is what's bringing in the most money. Ticket sales for that have already gone crazy. Once I add you? Whew, look out. Although once I post pictures of you and Aaron for the dating show portion, it will get more attention. Who wouldn't want to see men like you paired off? Hell, who wouldn't want to *be* paired off with men like you? You're fucking hot."

Dekker blushed slightly at the compliment. He didn't see himself that way, and he was continually amazed that other men did. His brown hair was cut in layers and hung to his shoulders. He had hazel eyes, and he was muscular, but nothing about his appearance in the mirror stood out to him. He worked out because it was a great stress reducer for him, and he liked how he felt when he finished. The bonus was that other men found his body attractive.

"Thanks," Dekker mumbled and took a sip of his iced tea to hide his sudden discomfort. He hated being the center of attention, and he had just agreed to put himself in the spotlight. He already regretted it.

"Come on, Dek. You're going to be in jeans, a cowboy hat, and nothing else at the dating show. Is it really going to matter that you're shirtless and in leather pants for the modeling show?" Alek leveled a look usually reserved for children. "Josh and Logan are doing it, and Rex and Justin."

That was the best Alek could come up with? Everyone else was doing it? Dekker closed his eyes, quietly sighed, and nodded.

"So you'll do it?" Alek asked.

"Yes," Dekker grunted.

"Excellent. I'm so excited. I'll email you all the details tonight. Thank you so much."

Alek pushed out of the booth, clapped his hands, and grinned like an idiot. He leaned down and kissed Dekker on the cheek and then practically skipped out of the restaurant.

Dekker took his time finishing his tea. He looked out the window at passing pedestrians and wondered why he hadn't been able to make things work with Alek. They had tried dating twice, but it just never went anywhere. Alek had told him both times the "spark" was missing. Dekker was beginning to think the "spark" didn't exist, whatever the hell it was. He left enough cash on the table to cover the bill and a healthy tip and headed for the gym. He had some serious nervous energy to work off this afternoon.

Chapter Two

Dekker stood in front of the three-way mirror staring at his reflection but not really comprehending. Chaotic activity had swallowed him up the moment he set foot in the community center. Alek's fundraiser had drawn quite the crowd. Every seat in the lobby was filled. Several friends of his were also taking part in the modeling show, but he was the only one dreading it. Everyone else seemed to be swept up in the excitement. Logan and Rex were standing a few feet away near the makeup table, chattering away about all the hot asses around. Dekker felt like he was staring at an oncoming train. Justin and his identical twin, Josh, walked over to their boyfriends who quickly shut up.

Josh smacked Logan on the shoulder. "Don't even pretend. I know you're looking."

Logan pulled Josh into his arms. "Yes, but I'm going home with you. Always, you," he said. Holding Logan's gaze, Josh leaned in closer.

"I know," Josh said softly. He ran a hand through Logan's short raven hair, tousling it and making it look like Logan had just rolled out of bed. "Better. Gotta make these boys jealous."

Dekker nearly jumped out of his skin when a warm hand pressed against the bare skin of his lower back. He had been watching the exchange between Josh and Logan, once again wishing he could find that kind of love. He had completely forgotten where he was for a moment. He caught Justin's gaze in the mirror just as Justin pressed his chest against Dekker's back and slid his arms around his waist, resting his chin on Dekker's shoulder. They were both shirtless and wearing scandalously tight, low-hung pants. Dekker stiffened and glanced at Rex just a few feet away.

"Relax, Dek. You look great," Justin said.

"There are hundreds of men out there," Dekker said.

He fisted his hands at his sides and then stretched his fingers spasmodically. The closer the time got for him to walk out onto that stage, the more nervous he got. His heart was pounding. He felt hot, and his breathing was shallow.

"You won't be able to see any of them. The lights will be low over the audience, and the spotlight will blind you," Justin said. He grabbed hold of Dekker's belt loop and tugged him around to face him. "Just walk to the edge of the stage, strike a pose, turn around, and walk back. No biggie."

"I'm half naked," Dekker whispered. He really, really did not want to do this. He wasn't shy, but he wasn't an exhibitionist either. Justin glanced behind Dekker and gave a pleading look. Dekker turned to see Rex joining them, carrying a leather vest that matched Dekker's pants. Rex handed it to him, and Dekker pulled it on. The vest left his arms and a good expanse of his chest uncovered. It stopped just below his navel, but the low-riding leather pants were a good inch or two below that. He still felt exposed.

"Better now?" Rex asked.

"Not really. But honestly, I could walk out there covered head to toe and still be uncomfortable," Dekker admitted.

"Why? You're a beautiful man," Josh said. Logan had taken a seat on the tabletop, and Josh was nestled between his legs, Logan's muscular arms engulfing the slimmer man. All four of his friends were watching him, waiting for his answer.

"It's not about my body. I know I look good. It's just walking out there and having hundreds of men I've never met looking me up and down and...judging." Dekker rubbed his palms together and looked at the floor. He hated how insecure he felt at the moment.

"I'm glad you agreed to the dating show later. We need to find you someone who will prove to you how wonderful you are," Justin said and lightly ran his palm down the center of Dekker's chest. Dekker was always amazed at how freely the twins touched other men when their partners were right there.

"Places, gentlemen, places," Alek yelled over the din of voices.

The men taking part in the modeling portion lined up in their predetermined positions. Justin caressed Dekker's cheek. He smiled and winked as he and Josh made their way to their spot in line. The twins would be going out together wearing worn denim jeans and nothing else. Their dirty blond hair and blue eyes, combined with their flawless fair skin and toned muscles, always caused a stir. Rex and Logan took their spots behind the twins. They were wearing workout pants, tennis shoes, and tank tops that showed off their impressive biceps and tattoos. The men were big and totally ripped. Dekker stood frozen in place. He was supposed to be after Logan, but he couldn't make his feet move. Alek walked up and offered him a slight smile. He put one hand on the back of Dekker's neck, slid the other into his hair at the back of his head, and pulled Dekker's forehead to his. Dekker held the other man's waist like a lifeline.

"You're going to be fine," Alek whispered, looking into Dekker's eyes. "I really appreciate you doing this. Do you know the number of men wanting to sign up for the dating show tripled after I posted that you were one of the eligible bachelors? You're a hot commodity, baby."

"That's not helping," Dekker said as his pulse began thundering in his ears. Alek chuckled and pulled away, letting his hands drop to Dekker's shoulders. He ran his hands up and down Dekker's biceps.

"Piece of advice—give yourself tunnel vision. Keep your eyes on the guy in front of you. Don't look around. Maybe pretend you're walking into the bedroom for a little hanky-panky, and your boy is on the bed. You want to impress him, turn him on, and make him all hot and bothered. When you get to the end of the stage, give your best 'come fuck me' look and then turn around and walk off," Alek said.

Dekker was so focused on not hyperventilating and listening to Alek's words that he hadn't realized Alek had walked him to his place in line. Alek swatted him on the ass and walked away to see to the other men lagging behind. Logan looked over his shoulder at Dekker and then moved up to whisper in Josh's ear. Josh looked back at Dekker and smiled before coming back and plastering himself to Dekker's chest. Before Dekker could process what was happening, Josh was kissing him, slipping his tongue into Dekker's mouth, nipping at his bottom lip. As quickly as he'd thrown himself at Dekker, Josh just as swiftly returned to his spot in line beside his brother. Dekker was completely thrown off balance. That had to have been one of the fastest, most distracting kisses Dekker had ever experienced. Logan chuckled and Dekker stared at him, dazed.

"You're welcome," Logan said.

Dekker followed the line as it progressed, vaguely aware of being nudged from behind when it was his turn. He was still completely distracted by Josh's kiss and the fact that Logan had put him up to it. How secure did that relationship have to be for that to happen without any kind of backlash? And Dekker knew there wouldn't be any. He was envious as hell. None of his past boyfriends had been that trusting. It was exactly the kind of love he wanted.

It wasn't until he'd reached the end of the stage that he was yanked back to the present by an explosion of catcalls and applause. Rex and Logan were flexing their muscles as they passed him on their way back. Insecurity swamped him, and he tucked his hands into his pockets, smiled shyly, and then turned and made his way to the back of the stage. He cast one last quick glance over his shoulder at the darkened room before dodging backstage.

The second and third times he went out were easier, though no less uncomfortable. He was convinced Alek had chosen the most outrageously scandalous clothes for him to wear. Now, Dekker once again stood in front of the mirror and waited for the dating portion of the evening.

"You did good," Alek said and kissed Dekker on the shoulder. Dekker turned around to stare at the man who, until tonight, he thought was his friend. After seeing the clothes Alek had him wearing, he wasn't so sure anymore. He held his arms out.

"Seriously, what is with the clothes?" Dekker asked. "I feel like a buffet set out in front of starving men."

"Oh, darling, if only you knew how true that analogy is," Alek said with a laugh.

Dekker let his arms fall to his sides. Alek had him wearing torn jeans, cowboy boots, a too-small denim shirt with the sleeves rolled up over his biceps, and a cowboy hat. All the buttons had been removed from the shirt so Dekker couldn't close it over his chest if he'd wanted to. And he very much wanted to. He felt exposed.

"I have to tell you, Dek. You looked smoking hot out there, and that shy act on stage has bears and twinks alike wanting to be the one to draw you out. You and Aaron are the bachelors, but there are four men for each of you on the other side of those barriers. You don't know what they look like, but they were in the audience for the modeling show so they know what the two of you look like. I can promise you, all eight were hoping like hell it was you they got a shot at," Alek said. He looked Dekker over from head to toe. He must have liked what he saw because his smile was blinding. "Damn, man. The money you brought in..." Alek pursed his lips and rolled his eyes heavenward.

"Great. Now I feel self-conscious *and* cheap," Dekker told him.

"Don't sell yourself short. You brought in thousands of dollars in donations."

Dekker's eyebrows lifted in surprise. Thousands? He turned to look at himself in the mirror again. He didn't see whatever it was these men obviously saw. He was handsome, he knew that, but there were plenty of men who looked better. He had just shared a stage with twenty-three of them. Pushing his confusion aside, he focused on the upcoming dating show. There would be no disappearing quickly with this one. He would be sitting in a chair in the middle of the stage in front of hundreds of men while he and four others he couldn't see asked questions of each other. He turned away from the mirror as Alek ushered him toward the stage for yet another humiliation.

"So, what kinds of questions can I expect?" he asked.

"Anything goes," Alek answered.

At Dekker's panicked expression, Alek laughed, clapped him on the back, and walked out onto the stage. The only rule he had given Dekker earlier was that he wasn't to look at the stage while Alek was introducing the four men hoping to "win" a date with him. It was an easy rule to follow. Dekker couldn't look in the direction of the stage at all and manage to remain calm. Justin, Josh, Logan, and Rex stopped by to wish him luck, staying with him until he was called out. He tried to focus on his friends as he listened to Alek whipping the crowd into another crazed frenzy. Dekker was apparently the favorite of the crowd, so to make sure the majority of people stayed the entire night, Alek had put Aaron's portion of the show on first. If the noise level was anything to go by, everyone had waited around to watch Dekker choose a man. It sounded like the place was still packed.

Alek brought out all four hopefuls at once. He introduced them to the crowd and instructed them to take a seat, any seat. He listened to the men's names with little interest: Jack, Brandon, Slade, and Randy. He had no idea what each man looked like because Alek had been very careful to keep him and Aaron separate from the eight men. He also knew the order of the names wasn't indicative of the contestant numbers. The men were given their numbers after they randomly chose their seats. In a matter of minutes, it was Dekker's turn to be introduced. He glanced nervously at his friends who all smiled excitedly and gave him the thumbs-up.

Dekker kept his eyes locked on Alek as he walked onstage to exuberant applause and whistles. He shoved his hands into his pockets and shifted nervously from foot to foot as Alek made him sound like an oversexed Thor. He ducked his head to hide his blush behind the cowboy hat. He really wished Alek would just shut up. There was no way Dekker could live up to the expectations Alek was creating. He glared at Alek as he was escorted to his seat. Alek chuckled softly as he took his seat beside Dekker.

"Keep your head up and the hat back. These people paid to see that gorgeous face of yours. Don't disappoint," Alek whispered.

Dekker blew out a nervous breath and did as he was instructed. He wanted to fidget. He wanted to try to close the shirt over his exposed chest. Somehow, he managed to remain still.

Alek lifted the microphone to his lips while watching Dekker from the corner of his eye. "Contestant one, what would you like to ask our bachelor?"

"Well," said a disembodied voice from the other side of the barrier. "Like everyone else here tonight, I like to have a lot of sex." *Great, contestant one was a player*, thought Dekker. "I'm curious what kind of stamina you have? Can you manage multiple orgasms in one night?"

Dekker groaned to himself as he slid sweaty palms over his denim-clad thighs. "Yes, I can," he answered. Applause erupted in the audience, and he shot Alek a pleading look. This was beyond uncomfortable. Alek smirked as he continued on.

"Contestant two, what's your question?"

"Yeah, I prefer experienced men, so I'm wondering when you lost your virginity?" came a voice that was higher and younger than contestant one.

Dekker took a deep, fortifying breath. When he had lost his virginity said nothing about his experience level, but whatever. "Fifteen with a girl, eighteen with a boy," he answered. He dipped his head down to hide the embarrassment, but a gentle nudge to his ribs from Alek had him raising his head again.

"Okay, contestant three, your turn," Alek prompted.

"I have to admit, I'm eager to see you naked. How many dates would I have to get through before that happened?"

Contestant three's voice was deep and gravely, like a smoker's, with a slight southern drawl. Dekker caught Alek's eyes. He imagined Alek was eager for that answer, as well, since they'd dated for months without it ever progressing to the bedroom. He scrubbed his face with both hands before answering.

"Um, I don't know. Depends on the connection, I guess," he answered. He'd had sex on a first date, but also never had sex at all with some men despite dozens of dates. Alek shook his head.

"Man of few words. Contestant four, you're up," Alek said.

"What would a first date with you consist of?"

Dekker shifted in his seat. Contestant four's voice was warm, husky, and slid over him like honey. His entire body took notice. Damn, the man's voice was sexy. He didn't realize his thoughts had drifted until Alek addressed him over the mic.

"Dekker, what's your answer?"

Dekker rushed to cover his sudden distraction and arousal by clearing his throat. He'd never been turned on by just a voice before.

"Sorry. I was thinking," he said and once again scrubbed his hands down his pants. "There's this indoor skydiving place that I've always wanted to try, so we'd do that first. After that I'd take you to the Tibetan restaurant I like. Then...I guess we'd decide if we still like each other's company and go from there."

"Wow. That's certainly different," Alek said with a smile. Dekker shrugged. "So what question would you like to ask your hopefuls?"

Dekker had known this was coming. Alek had told him that each man on the stage was allowed to ask two questions. Where he was expected to answer eight different questions, two for each contestant, all four contestants would be answering the same two questions from Dekker. He had complained to Alek how unfair that seemed considering he was the one who was supposed to pick a man. These guys would know more about him by the end of the game than he would know about them. Alek's response was to "make the questions count." He had also told Dekker that it was deliberately skewed so that Dekker would make the man he chose feel more special on the obligatory date because he would want to know more about him. Dekker had spent the entire week leading up to this night trying to figure out what to ask so he could get the most information.

"What personality trait is the most attractive to you?" Dekker asked.

"All right. Contestant one, your answer," Alec said, lifting a brow and nodding slightly at Dekker.

"Bold and daring. I like my men to be adventurous in bed," the man answered.

Dekker suppressed the urge to roll his eyes. The guy was obsessed with sex. Dekker doubted his soul mate was on this stage tonight, but he already knew for a fact he would not be picking contestant number one.

"Contestant two," Alek prompted once the catcalls from the audience died down.

"I suppose it would be faithfulness. Can't be having my man sleeping around on me, know what I mean?" A mixture of boos and applause greeted the answer. Alek smiled and shook his head.

"Number three, you're up."

Dekker's body tensed the closer he got to hearing contestant four's voice again. For the first time since arriving here hours ago, he was actually excited about something. Was it bad that he wanted to choose number four right now based solely on the man's voice?

"I think it's a tie between honesty and faithfulness. Like my opponent here, I can't have my man lyin' and cheatin'.'"

Dekker had no idea what was happening on the other side of the barrier, but the audience laughed loudly and clapped. Dekker shifted in his seat uncomfortably. His nerves had been a stone in his gut all night. All it took was the promise of the deep, sexy voice of number four to transform those nerves into butterflies that suddenly took off in a flutter.

"Contestant four, what's your answer?" Alek asked. He watched Dekker squirm in his seat and lowered his eyebrows. Dekker forced himself to remain still, but he eventually started tapping one foot on the floor.

"I'm laid-back so I want someone who laughs a lot and doesn't take life too seriously. I can be ridiculous sometimes, and I joke around all the time. You've got to have a good sense of humor to be around me for any length of time."

Damn, Dekker liked that answer. He closed his eyes briefly as warmth spread through his body. He wanted to stand up and scream, "I pick number four," but he figured Alek wouldn't appreciate that. Dekker did his duty and answered three more annoying questions revolving around sex from the first three contestants. He kept his answers short which seemed to be irritating Alek. Dekker didn't care. He was pleased when contestant four's second question was just as good as his first.

"What do you think makes long-term relationships work?" number four asked. Dekker once again had to take a minute to think about his answer.

"My grandparents were married for fifty-eight years and my parents are still together after thirty-five so I know what long-term looks like, but if I had to pick a reason why it worked, I think it would be forgiveness, a refusal to give up, and unconditional love." Dekker watched Alek's smile spread across his face. Alek winked and lifted his microphone to address the crowd.

"All right, everyone. This is it, the final round before Dekker chooses his man. Contestants, this is your last chance to impress our gorgeous bachelor. Dekker, what's your question?"

Dekker's excitement grew exponentially. He couldn't wait to hear number four's answer to this one. "How would you describe yourself to a blind man?" he asked. A chorus of oohs and ahhs drifted up from the audience.

"Shit. That's a great question," Alek whispered to him.

"You said to make it count," Dekker whispered back.

"I did," he mumbled and then loudly said into the microphone, "Contestant one, answer."

"Tall, dark, and handsome. I'd also say I'm outgoing."

Applause once again rose to a deafening pitch, and Dekker wondered what the guy was doing. It was obvious the contestants were playing to the crowd. He completely discounted contestant two's and three's answers of muscular and hot respectively because they were as shallow and self-absorbed as the first. Finally, the moment Dekker had been waiting impatiently for: number four.

"I'd say I'm happy and driven. I do everything I can to keep myself in a good mood. I try not to let other people bring me down. If I want something badly enough, I'll work to the bone to get it and just as hard to keep it because nothing worth having comes easy."

"I want him," Dekker said softly as he gripped the arms of the chair. This guy was all about personality. He hadn't used a single word that would describe a physical trait, and that got Dekker all kinds of excited.

"Hold your horses," Alek said.

Alek stood up and moved to stand with the thin wooden barrier at his back. He addressed the crowd, turning to the contestants every so often. "What do you say we help Dekker pick his man?" he asked the crowd. "By applause, gentlemen, who thinks he should choose contestant number one, Brandon Geiger?"

The applause was loud and rambunctious. Several high-pitched whistles made Dekker close his eyes. All he wanted to do was get up and walk around the barrier to see number four's face. He really hoped the man was as pleasant to look at as he was to listen to. Dekker fidgeted in his seat as Alek took *forever* to get through contestant two, Randy Johnson, and contestant three, Jack Bills. The volume of applause coming from the audience didn't change no matter which of the four contestants' names were announced. It was a constant din that was unimportant. Dekker knew who he wanted: contestant four, Slade Gannon. He had been dreading the required date scheduled for next weekend, but now he was looking forward to it.

Unable to sit any longer, he pushed to his feet. His legs and back were stiff from the uncomfortable director-style chair he'd sat in the past half hour, and he naturally slid into a full-body stretch with his arms over his head. The volume of high-pitched whistles intensified, and Alek turned to look at him. Dekker felt his jeans slip a little lower on his hips and quickly reached down to pull them back up. The last thing he wanted to do was flash a room full of horny gay men.

"Whew, that was one hell of a sight, wasn't it?" Alek asked the crowd with a smile. "What do you say we find out which lucky man gets a crack at Dekker's sexy bod?" The noise never ceased, and Dekker was certain he'd be deaf come morning. "Contestants, you can head backstage now. You'll be able to hear Dekker's answer back there. Wouldn't want him to see the face of his chosen before the big night, now would we?"

What? Alek had neglected to mention that earlier. Alek must have known what Dekker was thinking because as Dekker walked over to the partition to peek around, Alek grabbed his arm and yanked him back to stand in front of their chairs.

"My, my, a little eager all of a sudden," Alek said into the microphone. Dekker couldn't tell if he was still playing the crowd or if he was talking directly to him.

"You didn't tell me I wouldn't get to see him until the date," Dekker accused. Alek gave him a sly smile suggesting he had, as suspected, done it on purpose. He lowered the microphone so his next words would be heard by Dekker alone.

"I didn't tell you because I thought if you knew how long this would draw out you wouldn't do it," Alek said in a rush. He lifted the mic once again and looked at the crowd. "Are you ready?" At the answering applause, Alek looked at Dekker. "Dekker Callan, who do you pick?"

"Slade, number four," Dekker said into the microphone Alek thrust at him. "And I want to see him now," he whispered when Alek took the mic away. Alek just shook his head and kept his arm solidly locked around Dekker's elbow.

"Congratulations, Slade Gannon." To the crowd he said, "Follow us on the Cleo Farnes Clinic website to see how Slade and Dekker's date goes. You'll also see the results from Aaron and Tony. We'll be checking in with the couples the following Sunday to get their thoughts on each other and their time together..."

As Alek gave his closing speech, listed the last-minute donation options, and thanked those who attended and made the night a success, Dekker pulled his arm free and made his way backstage, hoping to catch a glimpse of the other players. There was still quite a bit of activity backstage, and a lot of people milled about, talking. Several men came up to Dekker to say hello or to congratulate him. With meeting Slade foremost in his mind, his nerves had completely dissipated. Despite appearances during this whole thing, Dekker was not a shy man. He spoke to everyone who approached him, trying to identify his mystery guy by voice.

"He's not here, Dek," Alek said from behind him. Dekker spun to face his friend, hands on hips. Someone swatted his ass with a "Hey there, stud" and Dekker flashed a smile. The guy was good-looking, but his voice was too high to be Slade.

"Did Aaron get to see his man?" Dekker asked, suspicious that this was just Alek's way of torturing him.

"No, he didn't. All eight contestants agreed to leave as soon as the winners were announced," Alek said.

"But they got to see us."

"They got to see a *lot* of you. There was a reason you and Aaron were the most sexily and least-dressed men out there. I got to say, this change in you is nice but awfully sudden. What the hell's gotten into you?"

"His voice," Dekker said. He reached up and adjusted the cowboy hat on his head.

"His voice," Alek repeated softly.

"Yeah," Dekker admitted and felt the blush rise up his neck. He sounded ridiculous even to himself. "His voice turned me on, and I want to see if he looks as good as he sounds."

"Well, I don't think Slade sounds all that different from anyone else, but I can promise you he's gorgeous. Can you put a little trust in me here,

Dek? All the men I picked for you are men you'd find physically attractive. Though I will admit Slade was a last-minute substitute. The original guy came down with pneumonia and is in the hospital."

"What's he like? What should I do for this date next Saturday?" Dekker asked. His anxiety was making a comeback, and he rubbed his palms together.

"He's an artist or something. I don't really know him that well. Like I said, he was a last-minute addition. And you should do exactly what you told him you would do. Feed him Tibetan food and take him skydiving or whatever. Go get changed and head out, all right? I got to get the cleanup started." Alek pulled Dekker into a hug and kissed him just below his ear. "Thanks again for doing this tonight." Alek pulled back, cupped Dekker's face in his hands, and brushed a light kiss over his lips. He took off into a crowd of people around the donation table, and Dekker headed to the changing station to get back into his own clothes.

Chapter Three

Slade sat in his car outside the three-story building that housed Adventure Tower. Dekker had actually followed through on the first date he'd mentioned last week. Slade had assumed that Dekker was just blowing smoke to sound good for the audience, but the man had actually planned indoor skydiving. Slade got out of the car and entered the air-conditioned building. As he scanned the room for Dekker, he wondered if his date also planned on taking him to a Tibetan restaurant. Slade had never eaten Tibetan food before, and now that he knew Dekker had been serious, he was excited to try it. Slade pulled his sunglasses off when he caught sight of Dekker leaning on the circular desk that surrounded racks of flight suits. He was bent at the waist, resting his weight on his elbows, and laughing with the flirtatious girl behind the counter. The man was all kinds of delicious in jeans and a loose-fitting gray T-shirt.

Slade took a moment to get his guilt under control. George had come to the apartment the Sunday morning after the dating show and apologized, asking Slade for a second chance, which after a few hours of conversation Slade had agreed to give him. Everyone made mistakes. But this date had been obligatory. If Slade was chosen, he had to go on at least one date. George understood that and had been surprisingly accepting, and here Slade was ogling another man's ass. And firmly toned body. And thick thighs. And gorgeous face. Shit, Dekker Callan was the whole package.

If every answer Dekker had given at the show was true, then Dekker wasn't only a smoking hot body; he was a decent man, too. It was going to be a long afternoon for Slade if Dekker turned out to be everything Slade now suspected he was. Slade approached the counter just as Dekker let out a bark of laughter at something the female employee had said. The deep rumble sent shivers over Slade's skin. Slade sidled up alongside Dekker, making sure his arm brushed Dekker's muscular bicep. Dekker's smile slipped a little as he turned his head to look at Slade.

"Hi," Slade said. Being this close to Dekker made his mouth go dry and just about every intelligent thought flee his brain.

"Hello," Dekker said.

"I have to be honest. I really didn't think you were serious about taking me skydiving."

Dekker's answering smile was contagious, and Slade found himself smiling back. "I'd recognize that voice anywhere. Nice to finally meet you, Slade," Dekker said. He straightened to his full six-foot-two height and extended his hand to Slade in greeting. Slade accepted the handshake. "I tried to get a look at you during the show, but Alek interfered," Dekker added.

Damn. Slade had completely forgotten that Dekker wouldn't know him on sight. Alek had gone above and beyond to make sure the contestants saw the two bachelors before the show. He had even printed postcards with photos of the men and their names underneath with a few key vitals: height, hair color, eye color, hobbies. Slade should have introduced himself instead of just assuming Dekker would know who he was. He pushed the minor slip aside. No point in dwelling on it since Dekker knew who he was now.

"So, can I expect Tibetan for dinner?" Slade asked with a teasing grin. For a brief moment, he saw the same modesty Dekker had exhibited during the modeling show.

"Yeah, I love the place. They have great food. Unusual, but

delicious." Dekker toyed with his earlobe nervously.

Dekker returned his attention to the receptionist behind the desk. Slade stood by and watched him handle the details of getting them checked in and paid for and then followed his lead as they got set up in flight suits. Slade was distracted by Dekker's presence the entire time they sat in the instruction class. He was hyperaware of Dekker's body pressed against his on the bench in the airlock while they waited their turn.

The huge jet engine beneath the net roared to life and the instructor went out first to show everyone how it was done. Slade thought it looked easy enough until it was his turn. If it hadn't been for the instructor constantly grabbing his leg to keep him balanced, he would have spent his entire turn spinning and rolling and probably literally bouncing off the walls. By the time they had each taken three turns and gotten out of the suits, Slade's cheeks ached from all the smiling he had done in the past forty-five minutes. He felt giddy and had giggled like a kid the entire time. He preceded Dekker out into the warm afternoon sun. Slade slid his sunglasses on and waited for Dekker to join him on the sidewalk.

"So, I guess we're going to be sore tomorrow. They said to make sure we drink lots of water and take it easy for the rest of the day. Apparently, that's harder on the body than it looks," Dekker said as he pushed his way through the glass door.

Slade laughed and turned to face Dekker. "I don't care. That was a blast. I haven't had that much fun in a long time. How did you hear about this place?"

"I don't really remember, but it was the first thing that popped into my head when you asked," Dekker answered. "Do you want to ride with me to the restaurant or do you want to drive yourself?"

"Is it hard to find?"

"No. Right off Eighth and Cherry, facing the mall," Dekker said, pulling his keys from his pants pocket. Slade watched the man's hand the entire trip into his pocket and back. Something that ordinary should not have been erotic. Slade tried to remember the last time George had done something he found oddly erotic like that. He came up with nothing.

"I'll meet you there," Slade said. He would use the time alone to get himself under control.

"Okay." Dekker smiled and spun his key ring around his finger.

Slade moved to the driver's side of his Mercedes, keeping his eyes on Dekker the entire time he walked to his massive black truck. The man had a fine ass. He was a wet dream walking, and Slade didn't think Dekker was even aware of how good he looked.

Chapter Four

Dekker waited until Slade was behind the wheel of his car and then pulled his truck onto the road. He drove to the restaurant, keeping an eye on the rearview mirror to make sure Slade found his way without any problems. The skydiving tower had turned out to be a great idea as far as something fun and different to do for a first date, but it sucked for communication. There hadn't been time for them to really talk to each other. He planned to make dinner last longer than normal so he could take his time getting to know Slade.

Dekker had been momentarily stunned when Slade had approached him at the tower. The man was far more beautiful than he'd imagined, wearing tight white-washed jeans and a black T-shirt. Slade had short dark hair that was slightly longer on top and deliberately styled to look disheveled. Slade's soft-blue eyes were surrounded by thick, dark lashes and sparkled when he laughed. His voice was exactly how Dekker had remembered it: deep, husky, and sexy.

Dekker had spent the last week imagining what Slade would sound like in the throes of passion and when he climaxed. He pulled his truck into the parking lot for House of Nepal and willed his dick to behave. It was going to be a long, uncomfortable dinner if he spent the entire time rock-hard. Slade pulled his sports car in next to Dekker's truck, and they entered the lobby together. They were quickly seated in the back of the restaurant near the fireplace.

Slade sat across the table and smiled. "Nice little place. I've never had this kind of food before."

The waiter handed them menus and took their drink orders. Dekker grabbed Slade's menu before he could open it. "Do you trust me?" Dekker asked, waggling his eyebrows. Looking apprehensive, Slade set the menu on the table and shrugged.

"Sure. Why the hell not?" he answered.

Dekker described the type of food and spices used in Tibetan food. He wanted Slade to at least know what to expect. The waiter returned and Dekker ordered a soup with lamb, a noodle dish with yak meat, and a vegetable dumpling dish. He wanted to give Slade a little taste of everything.

"Yak, seriously?" Slade chuckled.

"It's surprisingly good," Dekker said.

House of Nepal was one of his favorite restaurants. He was suddenly very nervous that Slade wouldn't enjoy the food, although he did seem to be enjoying the atmosphere. Slade's eyes moved lazily over the décor and artwork. Dekker took a nervous swallow of tea. Now that he had Slade in a quiet place where they could talk, he was becoming anxious. There were so many things he wanted to know about his date he was having a hard time deciding what to ask first.

"So, tell me, what do you do for a living?" Slade asked, taking the decision away from Dekker.

"I own a...store," Dekker answered. He was never sure how much about his business he should divulge, so he stumbled a bit with his words. Slade caught the hesitation and motioned for Dekker to continue.

"That's pretty general. What kind of store?"

Dekker slid his palms over his thighs. "Okay, but don't judge. It's an adult store. I sell sex toys, videos, books, kinky outfits—that kind of store."

Slade looked thoughtful for a moment, and then his eyes lit up and he smiled. "Your name's Dekker Callan. Your store is Callan's Closet, isn't it? I've been there once. It was fun."

Dekker just nodded and sipped at his tea. He should have remembered that Slade had been given his name and a photo of him at the charity event. Dekker felt cheated and decided to even the playing field.

"I know you were given information about me prior to the dating show, but I wasn't given anything at all on the guys taking part, so I feel at a disadvantage. Tell me about you," Dekker prompted.

"Actually, we were only given your name and picture, and we were encouraged to check you out during the modeling portion. You're one hell of a handsome man, by the way." Slade looked down at the table and rolled his napkin around in his hands, refusing to meet Dekker's eyes when he admitted to that last part. He shrugged. "Anyway, my last name is Gannon, and I happen to own a business myself. It's an art gallery called Trendz. I also own The Cellar which sells only wine and appetizers. I recently had the wall separating the two knocked down and installed smoked glass dividers that can be opened or closed, depending on the event. During the day I usually keep them closed, but if there's a big art show going on, I close the main door to The Cellar and open the dividers so people can mingle between the two. Turned out to be a lucrative idea. And I am officially rambling so I'm going to shut up and eat." Slade ran his hands through his hair and laughed.

It was at that moment that Dekker pulled his eyes away from his companion to see the waiter carrying a tray with their meal. The waiter placed the dishes in the middle of the table, asked if they needed anything else, and then left quickly when they answered in the negative. As far as Dekker was concerned, Slade could keep talking all night long. Rambling or not, he absolutely loved listening to the man talk. He had wondered over the past week if Slade's voice had affected him so strongly because he hadn't had the visual, but he now knew that to be untrue. Even with Slade's stunning beauty directly across from him, his voice still managed to get Dekker hard.

Dekker watched Slade's face closely as he tried the food. He hadn't ordered much because he wasn't sure if Slade would eat any. Dekker expected his date to be timid in trying something as different as yak, but Slade took a full bite, smiled, and nodded. Once it was clear Slade liked each dish and was enjoying the meal, Dekker started eating. They shared all three dishes, simply dipping into whichever one they wanted.

"Not much variation in wine and appetizers, but what kind of art do you sell?" Dekker asked Slade between bites. Slade looked offended and then smiled wickedly. Dekker wasn't sure what he'd said to bring on the mixed reaction.

"Oh, baby," Slade said, and Dekker tried to be subtle as he shifted in his seat. Those two words had rocked his world and had his pants uncomfortably tight. He wanted to hear those words again in that sexy-as-sin voice once he had Slade naked and writhing beneath him.

"I'm going to have to teach you a thing or two." Slade's voice brought Dekker back to the present, though his words hadn't helped Dekker's situation. He would love for Slade to teach him a thing or two, though Dekker knew Slade wasn't referring to sex. Dekker was positive he was the only one trapped in that fantasy. To cover his unease, Dekker stabbed a piece of yak meat and popped it in his mouth. Slade continued speaking as if the world hadn't just tipped on its axis.

"There are so many variations of wine I can't even begin to list them all, and you of all people should know the variations food can take on," Slade said, indicating the spread between them with his fork. Dekker couldn't form words with Slade grinning at him like that, so he just shrugged and nodded in acquiescence. Slade winked at him and scooped noodles onto his fork. "It's okay. George is the same way. Whiskey and cheese is his idea of drinks and appetizers. The fancier stuff is lost on him. He at least tries to understand the artwork, but I know he really doesn't care."

Slade ate the bite of noodles. Dekker just stared. Who the hell was George? And why was Slade suddenly talking about him? One good thing came of it. Hearing Slade say another man's name had effectively doused Dekker's lust. Dekker must not have been able to disguise the change in his demeanor as well as he'd thought because Slade took one look at him and realized something was wrong.

"Are you okay?" Slade asked.

Dekker swallowed his quickly dying hope and smiled weakly at his date. "I'm fine," he said, wondering if the lie was obvious. He leaned his elbows on the table and attempted to make his voice light and casual, though he felt like a volcano was erupting inside him. He was angry, depressed, jealous, and annoyed all at once. And over a man he'd just met. The ridiculousness of that wasn't lost on him. "So, who's George?"

"Shit." Slade lowered his fork to the table. "Sorry. It didn't even occur to me what I was saying."

Slade put his elbows on the table and ran both hands through his hair in the first show of nerves Dekker had witnessed from him. Unsure why he felt the need to comfort Slade, other than he felt the loss of Slade's flirtatious smiles, Dekker rushed to put the man at ease.

"It's fine, really. I'm just curious who he is," Dekker said.

"No, it's not fine. I feel like such an ass. I *am* an ass, and I'm sorry. I should have told you, but I...just..." Slade took a deep breath and straightened, looking Dekker right in the eye. Dekker felt the blow coming but was appreciative of the fact that Slade was at least man enough to look him in the eye when he delivered it.

"George is my boyfriend, but here's the thing," Slade said and reached across the table to grab Dekker's wrist when Dekker leaned back in his chair. Dekker was ready to leave at that announcement, but he was

29

never one to turn down an explanation. He would give Slade the benefit of staying seated no matter how much he wanted to go home and lick his wounds. Slade slowly loosened his grip, but didn't let go completely. Dekker was aggravated that he was more focused on how Slade's hand felt on his arm than the fact that Slade was taken.

"We weren't together when I agreed to do the dating show," Slade said. "My roommate, Phil, got sick and couldn't do it, and Alek needed a replacement. George and I had broken up a few weeks before, and Phil thought it would be good for me to get out there again, so I took his place. George showed up Sunday, all contrite and looking as shitty as I had been feeling. He wanted a second chance and, I don't know, I agreed. Though sitting here now with you, I'm finding it hard to remember why."

Slade's hand moved up Dekker's arm an inch or so, sending tingles and heat all over his body. Dekker rolled his arm to softly caress the inside of Slade's elbow with the back of his fingers. Dekker approved of honesty, even if he didn't want to hear it, and Slade appeared to be sincere. Slade suddenly released his grip and put both hands in his lap, averting his gaze to the fireplace.

"Sorry," he said.

Dekker swallowed thickly. "Me, too. I was really hoping this was going somewhere."

Dekker and Slade both leaned back in their seats to allow room for the waiter to clear the table. He left the check on the table, and Dekker snapped it up when Slade reached for it.

"You paid for the skydiving. Let me pay for dinner," Slade said.

"No. I picked you and that is essentially me asking you out, so I'll pay." Dekker pulled his wallet out and slid his credit card into the holder.

"Maybe, but I'm the asshat. I want to pay for your dinner," Slade insisted.

The waiter took the leather holder from Dekker and disappeared through the beaded curtain, ending the argument.

"Next time," Dekker said. "You never told me what kind of art you sell."

Slade stared at him thoughtfully before looking down at his hands in his lap. "All kinds, but I lean heavily toward contemporary, modern, and edgy. I try to keep a broad list of artists who will appeal to the largest number of people. The whole idea is to move people through, get artists seen, and get their names out there."

Slade shrugged, having lost some of his earlier enthusiasm. Dekker knew it was because the boyfriend had become an invisible occupant at the table. He didn't usually think of himself as masochistic, and he didn't usually continue to chase men who were spoken for, but for some reason, the hope that he would eventually have Slade wouldn't completely leave him. This was George's second time around with Slade. While Dekker hated the idea of Slade with another man, he figured it wouldn't last. Whatever had broken the pair up in the past was bound to happen again. It was a horrible thing for Dekker to hope for, and he knew it.

The waiter put the leather holder on the table and walked away. Dekker signed the receipt and left a generous tip, while his determination to wait for George to screw up again grew stronger. They stood, and Dekker motioned for Slade to lead the way out. Out on the sidewalk, Slade stopped and turned. He had his hands in his pockets and shifted nervously on his feet.

"Thank you for listening and not getting angry about George."

"Oh, I'm angry," Dekker said, catching Slade's gaze. "I'm more than a little pissed that you're with someone, but I enjoyed the afternoon all the same." Dekker pulled out his wallet and retrieved one of his business cards. He offered it to Slade, who accepted it with obvious confusion. "Call me sometime. We can still hang out."

"Damn, this sucks. I like you, a lot," Slade said.

Dekker shrugged, grinned, and walked around the front of his truck. If Slade liked him enough, he would dump George on his ass and seek Dekker out. And Dekker had every intention of seeking Slade out. He knew the name of the man's businesses and planned on looking them up when he got home to learn everything he could about them and their sexy owner. Dekker watched Slade battle with himself from the corner of his eye. He smiled inside when he saw Slade give in.

"Dekker, wait up," Slade said as he came around the hood of the truck. Dekker crossed his arms and leaned against the door. "I'm not...maybe we..." Slade faltered for only a moment before pulling it together. "Do you want to go dancing? Silver Linings is having this promotion thing tonight with pro dancers. Thought you might like to go to a meat show where you aren't the prime cut."

Slade gave Dekker that wicked grin that made his blood heat, and Dekker couldn't stop the laugh that bubbled up. Dekker peeked at Slade through his lashes and ran a hand over the top of his head.

"Good analogy. That's actually what it felt like, you know. Like I was a piece of meat those boys couldn't wait to sink their teeth into," Dekker admitted.

"Well..." Slade started, but cut himself off immediately. The way his eyes moved over Dekker from head to toe told Dekker exactly what he was thinking. Slade found him attractive, probably wanted to take a bite out of Dekker himself, and Slade had admitted that he liked him. Warmth spread through Dekker's entire body—everywhere Slade's gaze touched. Dancing in close proximity to Slade had to be the worst idea and the biggest threat to Dekker's honor. Slade belonged to someone else.

"Sure. Let's go dancing," Dekker said before he could talk himself out of it. By the time this night was over, Slade would know exactly where he stood with Dekker. And would know precisely the kind of relationship Dekker wanted to have with him.

Chapter Five

Slade pulled Dekker by his hand through the crowd amassed at the bar toward the slightly less crowded dance floor. He ordered two beers from a passing waiter and told the man where to find them. Slade was moving to the music the instant his feet hit solid wood flooring. He loved dancing, but George wouldn't be caught dead in a place like this. It was one of the reasons he'd asked Dekker. The other reason was that he wanted Dekker to himself, to feel his arms around him, to live this fantasy just a little longer.

If he'd known a week ago that Dekker was more than a handsome face and hot body and would turn his crank as hard as he did, Slade would have told George he'd lost his chance. Why he'd taken the cheating bastard back was beyond him at this moment. Slade would bet any amount of money that Dekker wasn't like that. Dekker would be loyal and faithful and love the man in his life with everything he had. Dekker had already asked more about Slade's life and business than George ever had. How sad was that?

Slade closed his eyes as the hand he was holding disengaged from his fingers to find his waist. Strong arms encircled him and a hot, hard body pressed against his back. He felt Dekker's erection against his ass as the man moved perfectly in time with Slade's dancing. The song had a fast Latin beat, and Slade rolled his hips, loving the feel of Dekker's body and prominent arousal pressed against him from behind. Slade placed one hand on top of Dekker's at his waist, threading their fingers together, and reached his other hand behind him to pull Dekker's head forward. Dekker lowered his head without argument and buried his face in Slade's neck.

The song ended, and Dekker pulled away slightly, but still maintained his hold on Slade's waist. The waiter found them on the dance floor, and Dekker took the beers while Slade pulled a twenty from his wallet and handed it to the server. He accepted his beer from Dekker and took a long pull. Slade was in so much trouble right now. He wanted Dekker badly, but Dekker deserved to be the center of his lover's attention, not just a piece of ass on the side.

Dekker drank his beer quickly, took Slade's from him, and discarded the bottles on an empty table nearby before pulling Slade back into his arms. Slade slipped his arms around Dekker's neck. Dekker led them in a slow dance despite the fast-paced music blaring around them. Each step caused their pelvises to grind against each other, moving their erections up and down and across one another. Slade pulled Dekker's head forward so their foreheads touched. Damn, he liked being close to Dekker like this. Slade liked the fact that he was the only one Dekker had eyes for, that he was the only one Dekker was dancing with.

Dekker's hands slid south over Slade's butt and then one slipped back up under Slade's shirt. Slade's skin was on fire where Dekker's palm massaged. Slade pushed his hips forward, seeking out more of Dekker's hardness. The man was an addictive drug. The more of him Slade got, the more of him Slade wanted. Dekker gripped Slade's ass and pulled him tighter against his body. Slade lifted his eyes to Dekker's molten hazel gaze. He licked his lips, and Dekker's eyes dropped to his mouth. Dekker groaned and kissed him, hard. Slade opened his mouth to Dekker's assault, and the kiss deepened, tongues battling for dominance.

Both men came to their senses at the same time, and they pulled apart. Dekker kept his hands on Slade's waist, and Slade held onto

Dekker's elbows. Both of them knew the line they had just crossed, but neither was willing to stop touching the other. Dekker pulled Slade back into his arms, and they started dancing again, though this time there was a distance present that had been missing before.

"Fuck," Dekker said in his ear.

"Yeah." Slade had no words for what just happened between them, but "fuck" seemed to sum it up well.

"Damn it, Slade," Dekker shouted over the music and grabbed Slade's face with both hands. "Why do you have to be so damn perfect and fuckable and taken?"

Dekker released Slade and moved away. He disappeared into the crowd, leaving Slade to wonder what the hell he was supposed to do. He was already halfway across the room, closing the distance to Dekker, before he realized he was chasing the man down. He caught up to Dekker just as he leaned over the bar and yelled an order for two beers to the bartender. Dekker raked his hands through his long hair and took slow, measured breaths. He wasn't sure his presence would be accepted, but Slade pushed in beside Dekker anyway.

"I'm sorry, Dekker. I didn't expect any of this," Slade said when Dekker turned his head to look at him. He dropped his forehead onto Dekker's shoulder. "God, I'm sorry."

"It's not your fault, handsome. We just can't do that again," Dekker said near his ear.

"I know."

"Here." Dekker pressed a cold beer into Slade's hand. Slade lifted his head and looked into Dekker's dark hazel eyes. "One more drink and one more dance, and then we go our separate ways. Because if we stay together much longer, I'm going to take you home and fuck you, and boyfriend George can take a flying leap."

Not wanting to take a chance that he would say something he

shouldn't, like "Forget George, just fuck me," Slade picked up his beer and drained it in one long rush. It was getting late, and he had promised George he'd call when the date ended so he could come over. It had seemed like a solid plan two days ago. Now, Slade was wondering how the hell he was supposed to spend the night with George after having spent the best evening of his life with Dekker.

Dekker finished his beer just as quickly, and Slade allowed himself to be pulled back onto the dance floor. Dekker once again wrapped him in a strong embrace and danced slowly despite the heavy beat and fast pace of the song playing. Slade allowed himself to get lost in the warmth of Dekker's arms and enjoy the feel of the man's body against him while it lasted, though the moment didn't last as long as Slade would have liked.

At the end of the song, Dekker pulled away, and the stage at the head of the dance floor lit up. Slade had gotten so caught up in Dekker that he had completely forgotten they were here to see the professional dancers, aka strippers. He hadn't told Dekker that little piece of information, and he now wondered what Dekker would think. For some reason, the idea of Dekker watching other men strip made Slade's gut churn. If this was how Dekker was feeling about Slade being with George, Slade could well understand why the man was so upset with the situation.

The first of the dancers came out on stage, dressed like a cop. He swung a pair of handcuffs on one finger, smiling wickedly at the crowd. He tossed the cuffs into the screaming mass of men. Dekker and Slade watched a group of four guys get into a shoving match over who would get the discarded handcuffs. Dekker turned to Slade. They stared at each other for a moment before erupting into laughter. Dekker returned his attention to the stage and watched the cop slowly take it all off as he moved to the music. Slade split his attention between the man stripping on stage and the man beside him laughing. Dekker smiled at Slade and pressed his mouth to Slade's ear.

"Is it always crazy like this?"

Slade laughed. It had never occurred to him that Dekker might be new to this kind of show, especially considering the type of store Dekker owned. Slade moved closer to Dekker under the pretense of being heard, but it was really just so he could feel the man's heat again. "Yeah, pretty much," he answered.

Dekker slid his hands around Slade's waist and then up to his lower back before pressing their bodies together. He leaned in close to Slade's ear so he could be heard. "We've got to stay for at least one more. This is too much fun."

Laughing, Dekker returned his attention to the stage as the cop finished his striptease. Slade ran his hands up Dekker's arms, loving the smooth heat of his skin, the bulges and ripples of muscles. Slade watched the next dancer take the stage but paid little attention to the man. His attention was completely focused on the areas where his and Dekker's bodies were touching. Slade let his imagination run wild and was lost in a fantasy of Dekker stripping naked for him when he realized Dekker was tugging him off the dance floor.

A table nearby had emptied, and Dekker pulled Slade to it with a firm grip on his elbow. Slade was enjoying the play of expressions on Dekker's face and once again found he was smiling nonstop. It was clear this was Dekker's first striptease, and apparently Dekker wasn't ready to leave. Dekker took a seat at the table facing the stage, and Slade slid onto the stool beside him. Of all the expressions Dekker was exhibiting, none of them were lust. Slade had been the only recipient of that look, and that made him go hot all over.

Slade once again mentally kicked himself in the ass. If he hadn't let the loneliness win out and taken George back, tonight could have been the beginning of a romance with Dekker that Slade had no doubt would blow his mind. Instead, he was once again in a relationship where he would question the fidelity and honesty of his partner. Dekker chucked him under the chin with a finger, bringing Slade's attention back to him.

"No frowning allowed, handsome," Dekker said with a smile.

"Sorry."

It was one word, but meant so much. He was sorry he'd led a great guy like Dekker on. He was sorry he'd lost control on the dance floor and kissed him. Above all, he was sorry he'd taken George back. Slade held Dekker's gaze, willing him to understand all of that without him having to say it. Dekker winked and then returned his attention to the firefighter on stage who had just thrown his pants into the crowd. Slade's heart skipped a beat at Dekker's playful happiness. He scrubbed his hands over his face. God, Dekker was hot. And Slade was a fucking idiot. Slade lifted his head when Dekker caressed the top of his head and slid his fingers through Slade's hair down to his neck where he squeezed gently. Dekker leaned toward him with an intent look on his face. Slade hoped he was about to be kissed again. He swallowed convulsively, and his mouth went dry. He very much wanted Dekker to kiss him again.

"It's okay. We"—Dekker motioned between their bodies—"are okay."

Slade nodded and pulled away, missing Dekker's touch immediately, but he had to put physical distance between them or he would end up straddling Dekker right here at the table and kissing him until they were both breathless. That was something he couldn't allow to happen. Slade refused to become that kind of man. He had a boyfriend. He had promised George a second chance, and he would give him one. Despite the fact that George had cheated on him, Slade refused to do the same to George. He wasn't that kind of man, and he knew in his heart that Dekker wasn't either. If Slade continued to disregard the fact that he was in a relationship by throwing himself at Dekker, Dekker might decide that Slade was unfaithful and not want him anymore.

Chapter Six

Dekker was having the time of his life. It sucked that it was with a man who was taken, but somehow that knowledge didn't diminish his enjoyment. He watched the strippers on stage take it all off and shake it like crazy for the men in the club. It wasn't so much the dancers he was getting a kick out of; it was the men in the crowd. It would never cease to amaze Dekker what a little alcohol and the pressure of a group mentality could do to some people. Age, race, height, weight, none of it mattered when there was an incredibly built, handsome man moving suggestively to the music in nothing but a thong that barely covered his jewels.

When the first stripper had come out on stage, Dekker had been prepared to leave. Halfway through the dance, he decided to stick around a bit longer and watch the crowd, and more specifically, Slade. He was extremely curious to see Slade's reaction since this had been his idea. Dekker had pulled Slade into his arms without even thinking about it. It was just so natural to have Slade pressed against his side. It was also an intensely satisfying experience to see that Slade paid little attention to anyone around them. His eyes had been glued to Dekker most of the time.

Score one for me, zero for Georgie boy, Dekker thought. He'd never thought of himself as mean, but damn, Slade's boyfriend brought out all kinds of feelings and ideas Dekker hadn't known he was capable of. Jealousy really was a monster, and the fact that Dekker was suffering it on the first date had him shaking his head. He really needed to end this night. He'd pushed it further than he'd originally planned already, but he couldn't seem to pull the trigger on the evening.

"We should probably head out," Slade said.

Dekker nodded. Slade had once again read his mind and beat him to the punch. Dekker stood and followed Slade through the crowd to the front door. Catcalls and screaming overpowered the music for a moment as another dancer took the stage. Dekker glanced over his shoulder to see a construction worker, complete with hard hat, begin his routine and smiled. Crisp night air greeted him as he exited the club behind Slade.

"Thanks for suggesting this. It was fun," Dekker said as they walked to the vehicles.

"Yeah, sure," Slade said. He stopped by his sports car and let his eyes follow Dekker as he walked around the hood of his truck. "Listen, Dekker. I really did have a great time today. You're wonderful, and I do like you, so I'm going to be honest and tell you that I don't think I can just hang out with you."

Slade fiddled with his keys. Dekker leaned his elbows on the hood of his truck and looked across at Slade. If Slade was uncomfortable or found it difficult to be around him, that was fine with Dekker. He actually liked the idea that Slade might be worried about things progressing between them if they were alone again because they just might. Slade didn't know it yet, but this was not good-bye. They would be seeing each other again. Dekker was already planning it. Dekker smiled and shrugged nonchalantly.

"That's okay. You're a whole lot of temptation yourself," Dekker said.

Giddy satisfaction coursed through his body when Slade adjusted from foot to foot at that comment and looked down at his hands. It did wonderful things to Dekker's insides to know Slade shared the attraction. That wonderful feeling quickly morphed into aggravation as the knowledge that if it wasn't for fucking George, Slade would be acting on that mutual attraction rather than giving Dekker the boot right now.

"What will you say tomorrow?" Slade asked softly without looking up from the keys in his hands. When Dekker didn't immediately answer, Slade lifted his eyes to look at him through his lashes.

"I'm confused," Dekker admitted.

"To Alek, when he does the follow-up tomorrow," Slade clarified, and Dekker resisted the urge to slap his forehead.

He'd completely forgotten about that part of this whole thing. Alek would be coming by tomorrow to do a quick video interview about their blind date. The video was going to be posted on the clinic's website so everyone who had attended the fundraiser the weekend before could see how it turned out. He briefly wondered how Aaron's date tonight had gone. Slade's husky voice brought him back to the conversation.

"On second thought, maybe I don't want to know."

Dekker watched Slade closely. The man was seriously upset over the whole boyfriend situation. Ridiculously enough, the guilt and remorse actually made Dekker like him more. Slade was most definitely the kind of man Dekker wanted in his life.

"I'll tell him it was a great blind date. We each tried things we hadn't done before, and it was a lot of fun. And I hope in the very near future there will be a second date."

"But George might see it," Slade told him. If there was supposed to be concern in those words, Dekker didn't hear it.

"I don't give a fuck about what George might see," Dekker said a bit more harshly than he'd intended. He had tried very hard all night not to let Slade see how much this whole thing had affected him.

"I know you don't," Slade said on a sigh.

"But you do, so I'll be careful what I say."

Dekker rapped his knuckles on the truck's hood and unlocked the doors with the press of a button on his key fob. "I'll see you around."

He didn't look at Slade as he got into the truck and turned the key. Dekker was careful to keep his gaze averted as he put the truck in gear and pulled out. If he looked at Slade now, he would never leave. Dekker would hate himself if he gave in to his urges and tried to fuck Slade tonight. He needed to get the hell away from the man right now.

★★☆

Three blocks later, Dekker pulled to the side of the road and threw it into park. He fished his phone out of his pocket and checked his text messages. The phone had been vibrating in his pocket nonstop since dinner, but he had ignored it. Five men were currently having game night at Rex's place and they all wanted to know how Dekker's date had gone. Dekker sent a short text to Justin that he was on his way. He shoved the phone back in his pocket and drove to the house where he would no doubt be subjected to an interrogation. The twins were ruthless when it came to getting information and gossip out of people.

Dekker parked in the street behind Alek's blue Honda. Rex's Jeep was parked in front of the garage, and Justin's bug was parked beside it. Parked at an angle behind them was Logan and Josh's Corvette. The car was the first thing the couple had purchased together after Josh had officially moved in with Logan. Josh frequently joked that instead of getting an engagement ring he got fancy wheels. Dekker made his way inside and found his friends gathered around the kitchen table, laughing and drinking. As usual by this time of night, the games had long since been put away, and it was down to socializing. Alek saw him first and got up to get Dekker a drink.

"So, how did it go?" Alek asked with a huge smile. He placed a shot of tequila and a beer in front of Dekker and sat back down. "He's one hot fucker, isn't he?" The question wasn't slurred yet, but Alek was definitely

46

relaxed. Apparently, the drinks had only recently come out.

Dekker's laugh was sarcastic. He knocked back the shot and chased it with a gulp of beer before answering Alek. The room was quiet, and all eyes were on him. "Yeah, he's hot. He's everything I look for in a man. And I want him...badly."

"See? I told you." Alek clapped Dekker on the back.

"You did," Dekker admitted. He could see Josh winding up with an onslaught of questions, so Dekker quickly cut him off. "But he already has a boyfriend."

The silence and facial expressions were comical. Dekker almost laughed except that telling his friends about Slade and boyfriend George, combined with the alcohol he was consuming, had him feeling depressed and lonely.

"What kind of guy does that?" Justin whispered, looking at his brother. Josh shrugged. Logan remained silent, though he held Dekker's gaze for a moment.

Rex reached across the table to pick up Dekker's shot glass. "Let me get you a refill," he mumbled.

"What do you mean he has a boyfriend?" Alek asked, breaking the silence. "It was a requirement that the men who applied for the date be single."

"He was at the time. They got back together after the fundraiser." Dekker rushed to ease his friends' growing anger. They would all take up arms against Slade on his behalf, but that's not what Dekker wanted. Slade was a great guy, and Dekker wanted his friends to like him.

"You know you're going to have to start at the beginning, right?" Rex said as he placed a full shot glass and the bottle of tequila in front of Dekker. Rex sat back down, and Justin was immediately leaning against him, Rex's big arm around him. Dekker wondered how long it would be before Justin moved in here.

"Yeah, okay," Dekker said and knocked back the second shot. He poured himself a third before starting. "First off, indoor skydiving is awesome. You all got to try it sometime. That had to be the best first date ever for me. We hit it off right away, I think. Slade was open to everything at the restaurant. He let me order for him. Sometime during dinner, while we were talking about his art gallery, he mentioned the boyfriend." Dekker paused long enough to polish off a third and fourth shot. "As we were leaving, I told him I was pissed that he had a boyfriend, but...whatever. He still asked me to go dancing. Big dumbass that I am, I said yes. But then I got him on the dance floor and holy fuck that was hot. That kiss nearly burned down the club."

"You kissed him? Even though you knew he had a boyfriend? Why would you torture yourself like that?" Josh asked.

"'Cause I decided I'm gonna steal him away. Fuckin' George ain't got nothin' on me."

Despite the fact that the tequila was already having a major effect on him, Dekker lifted a fifth shot and knocked it back. He drained the beer and felt the liquor turn his brain to mush. He was in a safe place with friends who cared about him. He was going to get drunk and let all his messed-up emotions over Slade and his own lonely life pour out of him.

"Damn," Logan said with a chuckle.

"Don't laugh," Josh admonished with a light slap to Logan's chest. "He's hurting."

"No he's not. He's plotting," Logan said and pulled Josh in for a kiss.

"Damn straight. Slade is mine. He just doesn't know it yet. I'm gonna fuck him so hard when I get him," Dekker said. Shit, this tequila was strong. Dekker was getting drunk fast. It was kind of like an out-of-body experience for him. Dekker was a spectator, watching himself knock back shots faster than he should and listening to the words coming out of his mouth, but he had no control over anything.

"Maybe I shouldn't have given him the bottle," Rex said as Dekker poured what had to be his seventh or eighth shot.

Dekker looked at Alek who was sitting quietly beside him. Alek was staring at him, but Dekker couldn't tell what he was thinking. His brain was fizzing out, and random thoughts and feelings struck him.

"Why didn't we work? I wanted us to work," Dekker slurred.

Alek's answering smile was slow, but sincere. "I know you did. I could tell. And I do love you, but you just aren't the one for me," Alek told him. "And I think you know I'm not the one for you, though it's pretty obvious to all of us that Slade might be." Alek motioned to Dekker's hands. He had the shot glass in one and the bottle of tequila in the other. "You've never reacted this way with other guys."

"This might be a bad time for me to say this," Justin said, looking Dekker in the eye. "But after you picked Slade, I kind of buddied up to him, and well, I invited him to the barbecue tomorrow afternoon."

Josh and Justin wore matching expressions of regret. The brothers had obviously concocted that plan together. Rex, Logan, and Alek shared quick glances before erupting into laughter. Dekker just let his head drop to the table with a loud thump.

"I'm so sorry, Dek," Justin said.

"It's cool, Justin. My head got heavy," Dekker said. The tequila was literally slamming him to the ground. He placed his hands on the table by his head, with the thought to push himself back up, but he couldn't seem to find the strength, so his forehead remained pressed to the table. He lifted one finger and waggled it in the air. "I'll start my seduction then. I'm gonna...I'm gonna eat food and make him wish it was him, and then I'll win."

"I don't think that came out the way he planned," Rex said. The statement was met with a chorus of no's. Dekker didn't think his words matched his thoughts either, but he didn't care. He was depressed, drunk, and suddenly very tired.

"It's almost two a.m.," Rex said. "We're all going to be here tomorrow for the cookout, so why don't you guys just crash here tonight? No point in going all the way home just to come back, right?"

"Sure," Alek answered.

"Great idea," Logan said around a yawn.

"Okay. Logan, help me get lover boy here up to a room. Justin, babe, mind cleaning up really quick?"

Dekker listened to the exchange but didn't really comprehend anything anymore. Seconds later, strong arms lifted him to his feet. He couldn't hold his head up, so he just let it hang to his chest as he was half dragged, half carried through the house. They cursed at him between laughs as they tried to get his help up the stairs, but Dekker couldn't seem to make his feet work. Eventually Rex and Logan got him into the first guest bedroom and unceremoniously dropped him on the bed. Dekker simply stayed where he landed. The two men maneuvered the blanket from under his body, yanked his shoes and T-shirt off, and then covered him with the blanket. Dekker was aware of everything taking place but couldn't seem to participate in any of it. He would open his eyes to slits, but then they would close despite his attempts to keep them open. A warm hand brushed Dekker's long hair back off his face.

"Hey, Dek. I know you can hear me, and you'll remember all of this in the morning, so I'm going to say something I want you to take to heart," Logan said. The warm hand continued to caress his head and neck. "We were in the audience while you and Alek were on stage. We watched your interest in Slade grow, and by the time Alek asked, we all knew you would pick him. Justin went backstage to catch him and chat him up before he left. But if Slade does have a boyfriend now...Dekker, you don't go halfway with anything. You meet a guy, see a potential future, get your hopes up, and go all out for him, and then you get hurt because it doesn't work out. Don't do that with Slade, please. Don't get your hopes up and put effort into a man who isn't available. That's a heartbreak you can avoid."

"Come put me to bed," Dekker heard Josh say softly.

Dekker managed to open his eyes long enough to see Logan push to his feet at the side of the bed where he'd been squatting to talk to Dekker. Logan turned out the light, plunging the room into darkness except for the shaft of light from the hall streaming in around Josh at the door. Logan put his arms around Josh's waist and kissed him. Josh hopped up and wrapped his legs around the bigger man who then carried him to the room across the hall.

Dekker closed his eyes and hunkered down under the blanket. He listened to movement around the house and a door close softly down the hall. He had no idea where Alek was sleeping, probably on the couch in the TV room downstairs. Dekker's heart ached as he thought about Logan and Rex making love to Josh and Justin. He wanted the kind of love the couples shared. And it sucked big-time that he would meet the man of his dreams and still end up alone. A few minutes later, Dekker dropped into a drunken, dreamless sleep.

Chapter Seven

Slade had gone back into the club after Dekker drove off. He had whooped it up with the other boys and danced with anyone who asked while the performers on stage did their thing. He'd even kissed a few other men just to compare to Dekker. No one else elicited the same hot passion and fuck-it-all attitude in him that Dekker had. It pained Slade to think that he'd lost his only chance at such a great man, so he drank until last call. He stumbled out to his car, sat in the driver's seat, and dialed George's number. It took three attempts to get it right.

"About fucking time," George answered. "Where the hell have you been?"

"I've been drinking, and I need a ride," Slade said. If George was angry enough at having been kept waiting, he would leave Slade in the parking lot all night. George was always trying to prove a point or change Slade's behavior that way. It never worked, and George seemed to be clueless to that fact.

"Fine," George said on a huff. "I'll come get you, but only because I've been thinking about you all night." George's voice had gone low and husky. Apparently the ride home wasn't the only one Slade would be getting tonight. Having sex with George didn't appeal to him at the moment, and he wondered if it ever would again. That was part of what had pushed Slade to drink in the first place. After just a few hours with Dekker, he realized George didn't do it for him anymore.

While George could laugh at jokes, he wasn't humorous by nature. He would frequently tell Slade he needed to take things more seriously or stop acting immature. He was also possessive and extremely jealous and suspicious. Dekker on the other hand was relaxed, fun to be around, and had actually been interested in getting to know Slade as opposed to just getting him naked. George had started out that way. He'd made Slade feel attractive and special, complimenting him constantly and buying him gifts, but then he'd changed once they'd gotten serious. Dekker made Slade feel attractive and special in an entirely different way. Not to mention the man was sexy as hell. He used to describe his connection to George as opposites attract, and that might still be true, but George would never measure up to the standard Dekker set.

"Slade, damn it, how drunk are you?" George yelled over the phone. "Answer me."

"Sorry. What did you ask?"

"Where. Are. You?" George enunciated each word dramatically, and the tone raked across Slade's nerves.

"Silver Linings. I'm in my car."

"Seriously? You're just a few blocks away from me. Can't you just walk?"

Slade's temper snapped. "No, George, I can't walk. I'm fucking drunk. Jesus, if I'd realized that coming to pick up your boyfriend was going to be such a problem, I would have called Phil," he yelled into the phone. "On second thought, that's what I'll do. At least Phil cares enough about me not to leave me in a parking lot all night. I'm calling him."

"No, you're not. I'm already getting into my car."

"Fine, whatever."

Slade hung up the phone and leaned his head against the headrest. He was drunk and tired; his legs felt like putty, and his willingness to put up with George's shit had disappeared when they'd broken up a month ago. Slade's head hurt just thinking about the dung heap he'd created tonight. Dekker had tried to hide it, but he'd been irritated about

Slade having a boyfriend, and when he'd driven off earlier, he seemed angry and refused to look at Slade. The whole situation had Slade itching for a fight. He wanted to scream and kick and maybe punch something.

No, he thought a moment later. This was all sexual frustration brought on by Dekker. What Slade really wanted was a good, hard fuck...with Dekker Callan.

George chose that second to pull into the parking lot. He parked beside Slade's car, and Slade got out. He locked his Mercedes and slid into the passenger seat of George's sedan. The drive back to George's apartment was made in silence. Slade's thoughts were roiling in his alcohol-dazed brain, and George seemed willing to leave him alone for the moment.

At the apartment, George used Slade's unsteadiness as an excuse to touch him, rubbing their bodies together suggestively. Apparently George's annoyance at having to pick Slade up in the middle of the night had been short-lived.

"I've missed you," George whispered as he helped Slade into the bedroom. Slade stared at the bed as George's hands and lips roamed over his body. He felt like he was cheating on Dekker, and it instantly pissed him off. George was his boyfriend, not Dekker. Having sex with George was perfectly acceptable. Slade tensed in George's arms, and George misunderstood.

"I'm sorry, okay? I hated sitting here at home all day, knowing you were on a date with some other guy. I spent hours imagining all kinds of things, and the later it got, the more I worried."

Slade spun in George's arms to face him. He threw his arms around George's neck and kissed him. George walked him backward to the bed, and Slade pulled George down to the mattress on top of him. Slade shut his brain off and let his body take over. They separated long enough to undress, and then George was back on the bed with him. Slade knew all

55

George's moves, knew the routine he would follow, and Slade went through the motions of sex mechanically. His heart and mind weren't involved at all, even as George rolled on a condom, pushed his cock into Slade's ass, and pounded him into the mattress. Slade climaxed because it was the natural progression of what was happening. George's thrusts became erratic, and seconds later, he came with a yell. Slade felt George stiffen as he released deep in his ass and waited for his body to relax enough from his own orgasm for George to pull out. The sex had been good despite Slade's disconnection, but then sex had never been a problem for them.

"Shit," Slade breathed.

The edge had been taken off, and now fatigue slammed into him. George chuckled as he disengaged from Slade's body and rolled from the bed. Slade's eyes drifted closed as he watched George carefully remove the condom and enter the bathroom. He hovered on the edge of sleep when George returned and tugged him farther onto the bed and under the covers. Slade rolled to his side, facing away from George and settling in for the night. George spooned behind him and wrapped him in a tight embrace. Sleep came quickly.

Chapter Eight

Dekker woke slowly to the bouncing of the mattress. He groaned in pain as he rolled to his back. Every muscle in his body hurt like hell. He threw an arm over his eyes to block the sunlight streaming in through the open drapes and in a futile attempt to ignore the cute twink jumping on the bed beside him.

"Rise and shine, sleeping beauty," Justin said as he jumped once more and landed on his knees beside Dekker. "Rex says if you don't get up on your own, he'll come up with ice water and dump it on your ass. You know he'll do it."

Dekker groaned again and let his arm slide off his eyes to the pillow beneath his head. "Don't ever let me drink that much again," Dekker pleaded. He felt like shit. "I hate how I feel the morning after a drinking binge."

"It's almost one in the afternoon, Dek. You have to get up. People will start showing up soon. I volunteered to be the one to wake you up because I have to tell you something."

Dekker rolled his head to the side to look at Justin. The guy was attractive with that dirty-blond hair hanging over his forehead and clear-blue eyes that looked worried. "What?" Dekker asked, not entirely sure he wanted to know the answer.

"I called Slade this morning to see if he was still planning on coming, and he said he was."

"Okay," Dekker said, certain there was more.

"He asked if he could bring his boyfriend, and I thought it would be suspicious if I said no so I said he could. I'm sorry, Dek," Justin said desperately as Dekker rolled off the bed and got to his feet. This wasn't what Dekker wanted to hear immediately after waking up with a hangover, but it wasn't Justin's fault. Dekker leaned in and put his hands on the mattress, placing a soft kiss on Justin's lips.

"Stop worrying about it. I don't like the idea of George being here, but I'm looking forward to seeing Slade again. Can't win him if he isn't around." Dekker winked and rubbed his nose against Justin's as Rex appeared in the doorway. Rex leaned against the jamb and crossed his beefy arms over his chest. Justin grinned at his boyfriend from the bed as Dekker straightened.

"We're running away together," Dekker told Rex, dipping his head to indicate Justin.

Rex erupted into laughter. "Sure you are," Rex said as Dekker eased past him into the hallway. Dekker grinned widely at the slightly bigger man and then walked across the hall into the bathroom. He watched Rex take Justin under one arm and lead him downstairs before Dekker closed the door and started the shower. It was going to take quite the internal pep talk to prepare him for seeing Slade walk into Rex's house with his boyfriend in tow. At the same time, he was eager to meet his competition face-to-face. As Dekker was rinsing off, he heard the bathroom door open.

"Brought you some clothes and a toothbrush, Dek," Rex said. "Think everything will fit okay. Hurry it up, though. Stan and Greg are already here. And just so you're ready for it, Alek has decided to do the video follow-up with everyone while they're here. Aaron and his date, Tony, are coming, too. Told him he could set up in the office and do his thing with the four of you."

Dekker shut off the water, pulled the curtain aside, and grabbed a towel. Rex leaned against the far wall with his ankles and arms crossed.

He took in Dekker's body with a quick once-over and then looked back to Dekker's face.

"Two things: first, are you sure you're okay with Slade being here? Justin really didn't mean anything by it, which brings me to the second thing: don't ever flash my boy like this."

Dekker shook his head as he dried off. "I'm perfectly fine with Slade being here. Justin and Josh are sweet, loving guys who just want to see me hooked up."

Rex blew out a breath and nodded, clearly relieved that Dekker wasn't angry with his cute little boyfriend. Rex straightened and reached to open the door.

"By the way, I only let you see me naked because I know you don't care. I would never have done it with the twins or Logan. Hell, sometimes I think Josh and Logan would sandwich me between them if they thought I was open to it."

Rex smiled and cocked his head to the side as he pulled the door open. "Maybe. You'll do the shirt justice."

"What?" Dekker asked, but Rex left the bathroom chuckling, closing the door behind him, so Dekker finished getting ready.

He towel dried his long hair and then finger combed it back off his face. Rex had brought him jeans that were only a little loose around the waist and a green T-shirt. Dekker unfolded the shirt and laughed out loud. He pulled the shirt on, knowing it was just Rex's idea of revenge for Dekker kissing Justin. If seeing Dekker wear a shirt that read "All This And A Big Dick" in front of everyone made the big guy feel better, so be it. Dekker had a sense of humor.

Dekker headed downstairs and followed the sound of voices out into the backyard. He ran his hands through his hair a few more times to help it dry and joined the party. Rex met him at the door with a huge grin on his face and clapped him on the back.

"You're funny, aren't you?" Dekker said to his friend.

"Well I thought so until I saw you naked. Now it just pisses me off because I know it's true. Come on, grab a beer or something," Rex said.

Rex led him across the wooden deck where two coolers with ice held the beverages. Dekker grabbed a Corona and then went down the three steps to the grass to join Alek and the twins in the yard. He flopped down in the grass and smiled as the three looked at his shirt and laughed. Dekker ran a hand over his chest, smoothing the T-shirt.

"Your boyfriend decided to give me shit today." Dekker winked at Justin.

"Why didn't you just go into the bedroom and get another one? He has more than one shirt, you know," Justin said with a smile.

"Nah. I can play along. Besides, it's great advertising."

"Question then becomes is it false advertising?" Josh asked.

"Not even a little bit," Dekker said with a wicked grin.

Alek knocked the necks of their beer bottles together in a salute, and they both drank. It was a warm, sunny day for a cookout with friends. Dekker lay back in the grass and listened to Alek and the twins talk about gardening, cooking, and cars. The conversation was relaxed and flowed easily. The noise level rose with each new arrival, and Dekker caught himself looking around for familiar faces. He saw Aaron walk up to Logan who was preparing the grill, and Dekker pushed to his feet. Aaron saw him coming and waved. Aaron pointed to the T-shirt as Dekker joined him and Logan at the grill.

"Love the shirt," he said.

"Friend's idea of a joke," Dekker said. The men hugged in greeting. Logan dismissed himself to the kitchen to help Rex get the burgers ready, leaving Aaron and Dekker alone. They moved to stand along the deck railing to talk.

"How was your date?" Aaron asked.

"Fucking awesome except for the part where between the show and our night out he got back together with his boyfriend," Dekker answered. He shrugged at Aaron's surprised expression. "What about you?"

"Honest to God, it was awful." Aaron laughed hard.

Dekker was confused. "If it was awful why are you laughing?"

"Because it was just ridiculous. I picked him up at his place because I was trying to be gentlemanly and make a good impression. On the way to the restaurant my car broke down. Spent a good hour and a half with my head under the damn hood. We ended up eating at an all-night deli. Then we decided to go to a bar and play pool, and he took an elbow to the eye. We finished the night in the freaking ER. He had to get two stitches in his eyebrow, and he has a black eye."

"Jesus, man," Dekker said. He couldn't help but smile along with Aaron. The man's date had indeed been awful.

"I know, right? Tony's a great guy, though. He agreed to give me a second date so I could prove to him I really do know how to treat him right."

Aaron and Dekker fell into companionable silence as they drank their beers and soaked in the sun. Conversation and laughter filled the air. Dekker watched Josh and Justin have an animated discussion with a cute blond. He didn't see Alek anywhere, but he knew the guy was still around.

"Dek, man, you got a hottie checking you out."

Aaron spoke soft and low to keep his voice from carrying. Dekker followed Aaron's discrete pointing to find Slade watching him from the back door. Dekker smiled and lifted his beer bottle in salute. He took a long swallow of the brew when an older, handsome man walked up behind Slade and put an arm around his waist. The older man, who Dekker presumed to be George, pushed Slade out the door onto the deck. Alek walked up to the couple and greeted them. Out of self-preservation, Dekker returned his attention to Aaron.

"That hottie would be Slade, my date last night," Dekker said in response to Aaron's questioning look.

"Ah."

"Where's yours? I was told Alek would be doing the after-date show, or whatever, here this afternoon."

"Haven't seen him yet, but you'll know him from his injuries. Damn, I still feel terrible about that."

"Was it your elbow that took him out?" Dekker asked.

"Nah, some drunk guy the next table over, but still," Aaron said. They both polished off their beers and tossed the bottles.

"This sucks. You have the worst first date and get to see him again. I go out on the most kickass date ever, and the guy is unavailable. Just my fucking luck," Dekker complained.

Aaron watched Slade and George as they spoke to Alek. Justin had joined them in the few minutes Dekker's eyes had been averted. Dekker was hyperaware of Slade's presence, and despite not wanting to see George touching him, Dekker kept sneaking peeks at Slade. It seemed impossible for Dekker to keep his eyes off the man for long.

"Oh, I don't know, Dek," Aaron said and looked at Dekker askance. "Want my professional opinion?"

Aaron was a psychologist who specialized in relationship and couple's therapy. The man was incredibly gifted at interpreting body language, speech patterns, and word usage to identify the underlying issues causing the relationship to struggle.

"Absolutely," Dekker answered. "I plan on stealing Slade away, so it would be immensely helpful to know where the weak spots are."

Aaron stared thoughtfully at Dekker for a moment. "What? Slade is the one for me. I know he is," Dekker said defensively.

"Okay, well, I don't think you're going to have to steal him. Pretty sure you could just wait," Aaron said, returning his attention to the couple in question.

"Really? Why?"

"That relationship has problems. From the way the boyfriend is holding onto him, I'd say big problems. The embrace is too possessive and controlling, almost like he's afraid to let Slade out of his sight."

"He probably is. This is the second go for them," Dekker told him.

"I don't think it will last. Not if they don't address the trust issues between them. I'm guessing the boyfriend did something to break Slade's trust, and now he's overcompensating. It comes across as insincere and subconsciously Slade is aware of it. That's a relationship I would love to hear about from the inside," Aaron said.

"No. Don't go fixing shit, man," Dekker said. He didn't need Aaron going and helping Slade put his relationship with George back on track.

"Probably couldn't fix that if I tried. Slade doesn't want it."

Dekker couldn't stop the smile from spreading on his face. "What makes you say that?"

Aaron caught Dekker's gaze. He chuckled and shook his head. "He keeps looking at you. Does not bode well for the boyfriend."

Dekker looked over to the couple and caught Slade watching him. Slade quickly averted his gaze to Alek, who was talking with George, but it was enough to kick Dekker's heart rate up. "Do you think George knows?" Dekker asked.

"Oh, yeah, he knows," Aaron answered with a nod.

Something to Dekker's left caught Aaron's attention, and Dekker twisted around to see what it was. A tattooed, muscular guy with a bald head and goatee walked up to them. Dekker knew immediately who the man was because of the eyebrow sporting two stitches and the bruised eye. Dekker was caught off guard. For whatever reason, as he and Aaron were discussing their dates, Dekker had pictured Tony as a smaller, more effeminate man than Aaron, not an ex-con look-alike who could take on an entire biker gang by himself. Tony pulled Aaron into a hug.

"Don't freak out on me. It looks worse than it is," Tony said. He kept one arm around Aaron and extended the other hand toward Dekker. "Tony Harker."

"Dekker Callan."

They shook hands, but further conversation was quickly curtailed by Alek.

"Hey, let's get this postdate interview over with so we can enjoy the party. Come on." Alek motioned the three of them into the house.

Tony and Aaron held hands the entire time, and Dekker felt another surge of envy. Everyone around him was pairing off. Slade stood in the living room beside George, whose gaze was glued to Tony as he and Aaron passed by.

"Come on, Slade. George, you can hang here if you want. We won't be long," Alek said as he led everyone into the office. Dekker smiled when Slade waited for Tony and Aaron to pass so he could walk beside Dekker.

"I'm sore from the skydiving. How do you feel?" Dekker asked with a smile.

"I feel like it was worth the soreness," Slade answered.

They entered the office, and the four of them looked at the video camera behind the desk. Alek stepped behind the desk, out of range of the camera.

"Aaron, you and Tony are first. Sit right here," Alek motioned to two chairs set up across the desk from Alek, situated directly in front of the camera. "Dek, the two of you can just sit on the couch."

Dekker pushed a folded blanket and pillow to one end of the sofa and took a seat next to Slade. He used the items on the cushion beside him as an excuse to touch Slade's thigh with his own.

"This where you slept last night?" Dekker asked Alek. "Comfy."

"Yeah, it was either the sofa or sleep with your drunk ass," Alek said.

Dekker mumbled something unintelligible, and Slade jerked his head toward him.

"Were you drunk when you left last night?" Slade whispered. Alek was already giving instructions to Aaron and Tony while he prepared the camera. Dekker's attention was snagged completely by the man sitting against him. Slade's tone and expression were concerned.

"No, I was sober," Dekker whispered back. "And when I did get drunk, I was safe here among friends."

"Okay," Slade said.

Dekker got the sense Slade wanted to know more, but he kept a lid on his curiosity. Dekker and Slade remained silent so they could listen to Tony and Aaron recap their night together.

"First things first, thanks for playing along," Alek said and both men nodded. "I think the first question everyone has is what the hell happened to your eye?" Alek asked. Aaron groaned and closed his eyes. Tony laughed.

"Doc here got a little exuberant in the sack last night," Tony said.

"What?" Aaron and Alek asked at the same time. They both stared at Tony in shock. Already knowing the story, Dekker silently laughed. Slade looked at him questioningly. Dekker didn't say anything; he just held Slade's gaze and leaned back, kicking his legs out in front of him. He draped an arm over the back of the sofa behind Slade. If Slade leaned back, Dekker could wrap his arm around his shoulders. He really hoped Slade would lean back.

"I'm just kidding," Tony said and pulled Aaron against him with a muscular arm. "Some drunk guy at a pool hall caught me with his elbow."

The two men relayed their doomed first date for Alek and the camera. Slade watched and listened attentively. Dekker found he was grateful for that and used the time to study Slade. It had only been about twelve hours since he'd last seen him, but Dekker had missed him. Dekker felt more at peace and fulfilled when Slade was around. He'd noticed the odd reaction the moment Slade had stepped outside. Dekker turned his attention back to Aaron and Tony as Alek wrapped up the interview.

"Do you plan on seeing each other again?" Alek asked.

"Yes," Aaron said at the same time Tony responded with, "Absolutely."

"Can't leave him with that kind of first impression," Aaron clarified. "Bad for my rep."

All three men laughed. "Good luck to the both of you. Thanks again," Alek said.

He pushed the pause button and waited for the couples to switch places. Dekker heard the men talking as they took their seats on the sofa, but his attention was once again on Slade alone. Slade and Dekker watched each other as they sat in the chairs facing Alek. Dekker had no idea what to say, and it looked like Slade might be suffering the same indecision. Alek kept the camera paused as he addressed them.

"I don't even know how the hell to do this with the two of you," Alek admitted. "I mean, your date could be the beginning of a soap opera for crying out loud."

"It was a great date," Dekker said.

"But you did it backwards. They had an awful night, but they'll be seeing each other again, which is a happy ending. People will eat it up. You guys have a wonderful time, clicked right off, but no happy ending because Slade went home and fucked George."

Dekker glanced at Slade beside him and saw the flush creeping up over his face. Shit. Alek was right. Slade had ended his date with Dekker and then gone on to have sex with another man. Dekker shook his head and grabbed his jealousy in a chokehold. Slade and George were a couple, and they could have sex whenever they wanted. To hammer that point home, he told Alek exactly what he was thinking.

"They're boyfriends. They can have sex whenever they want. Just don't ask certain questions," Dekker said.

"I'm sorry," Slade said. Dekker knew he was apologizing to him, not Alek, and Dekker would have none of it.

"I told you last night, you have nothing to be sorry for," Dekker said to Slade. He returned his attention to Alek.

"Let's just do this already." Dekker raked his fingers through his hair in a last minute effort to look good for the camera. Slade leaned over to whisper in his ear.

"You look great, and thank you."

Dekker smiled and kissed him. "So do you," he whispered against Slade's lips. Kissing Slade had been a monumental mistake because the second their lips met, Dekker had tunnel vision. All he could see were Slade's beautiful blue eyes, and all he could feel was Slade's heat. Alek cleared his throat, and Slade jumped back. Dekker snapped his attention to Alek on the other side of the desk and noticed the blinking light on the camera. If that kiss had been caught on tape, he would have to get Alek to edit it out. Alek's shit-eating grin told Dekker the kiss had definitely been recorded.

"So, how was your date?" Alek asked with a wicked smile.

Dekker had to school his features not to scowl at Alek. "It was great. We're both a little sore from the skydiving, but we had a lot of fun," Dekker answered. At first the smile was forced, but as he thought back on last night and looked at the man beside him, it became genuine. He truly had enjoyed every minute spent in Slade's company.

"The food was interesting. I've never had yak before, but it was good," Slade added.

"Yak?" Alek asked. His tone reminded Dekker of being scolded by his mom as a child when he had disappointed her. "You fed the man yak?"

"Don't knock it till you try it," Dekker responded. "Lucky for me, Slade was open-minded and willing to try new things."

"Okay. So indoor skydiving and yak..." Alek seemed at a loss where to go from there. Dekker took pity on the man.

"I think my favorite part of the night was the strippers," Dekker said. That got Alek's attention. Slade barked out a laugh.

"Mine, too. I wish you could have seen the look on your face when that cop started taking it off," Slade told Dekker.

"I was just wondering if he was any good with the handcuffs," Dekker said.

"Or if he knew how to use his nightstick," Slade added, and they both dissolved into laughter at Alek's facial expression.

"Man with a body like that? He knew how to use all his equipment," Dekker said. "Did you see the hose on the fireman? That fire was only ten percent contained."

"Oh, good God," Alek breathed as Slade and Dekker once again erupted into laughter at his discomfort.

"I think it's safe to say the night was a success," Tony chimed in from the sofa.

Dekker tried to get control of his laughter. He was dangerously close to giggling.

"We should have waited for the construction worker to show us his nuts and drill," Slade said between breaths. Dekker held his stomach and slid down the chair a bit at Alek's flushed and scandalized face. His body had already hurt before Slade and Alek had sent him into hysterics; now he couldn't catch his breath.

"Okay, interview is over. Thanks for taking part," Alek said as he leapt from his seat to shut the camera off.

"That was interesting," Aaron said as he and Tony left the room. Alek walked around the desk to close the door behind them.

"All right, you two, pull yourselves together," Alek said. He stood beside Dekker's chair, hands on hips, as Dekker and Slade regained control. "Strippers," he muttered with a shake of his head.

Slade and Dekker exchanged smiles as they rose to their feet. Their lighthearted happiness was contagious, and Alek finally broke into a smile. A hard knock on the door grabbed their attention. Alek opened it, and George stepped into the office. His gaze slid over Alek and stopped on Dekker. Never taking his eyes off Dekker, George extended a hand to Slade.

"Let's go, babe. I need to get home," George said. The imperial tone and veiled demand had Dekker bristling. He narrowed his eyes.

"If you want to hang out a little longer, I can take you home later, Slade," Alek offered.

Apparently, Alek didn't like George's heavy-handedness either. Dekker appreciated Alek stepping in because he was currently in a staring contest with asshole George. Seeing the way George was treating Slade killed any and all guilt Dekker had suffered over the idea of breaking the relationship up. From this moment on, he was going after Slade full force. Dekker pretended George wasn't in the room and gave Slade all of his attention. Dekker loosely took Slade's other hand in his.

"Do you want a burger before you go?" Dekker asked.

Slade squeezed his fingers. "Thanks, but I do have to leave. I drove and there's a show at Trendz tonight. I have to get the gallery and restaurant ready to open, and I like to do a last-minute meet with the artist to discuss final placement of the pieces. Make sure everything is displayed the way they meant for it to be seen."

Dekker led Slade out of the room by the hand. He deliberately kept his grip loose and gentle so that Slade could break contact if he chose to. Dekker wanted the man to leave his boyfriend, but he wouldn't force the issue. Dekker was going after Slade subtly so that when Slade left George, it would be because Slade chose to. George stubbornly held onto Slade's other hand. Once out of the office door, Dekker released Slade's hand to caress his back. He walked them to the front door and placed a quick kiss on Slade's cheek.

"It was nice to see you again," Dekker said.

Slade smiled at him as he left the house, tugging George out behind him in an attempt to avoid further conflict between the men. Dekker's eyes turned hard as George yanked his hand free of Slade's and turned an angry glare on Dekker. The men faced off toe-to-toe in the doorway. Dekker felt Alek's touch on his lower back as he slipped his fingers through two of Dekker's belt loops. Alek would use them as handholds to yank Dekker away if the men came to blows.

"He's mine," George bit out through clenched teeth.

A million things to say flew through Dekker's mind, but in the end he decided to continue with his initial tact. Ignore the man. He looked over George's shoulder at Slade, who was watching the interaction with obvious concern.

"I'll be thinking about you, Slade," Dekker said with a smile and closed the door in George's face.

Chapter Nine

Slade turned away from George as Dekker closed the door in his face and fought to suppress a smile. He had known exactly what Dekker was doing the second he'd taken his hand in the office. Slade had been incredibly incensed at George's order, but hadn't had a chance to react before Dekker and Alek had jumped in. He found it was fun to see someone other than himself put George in his place. Slade was also turned on by Dekker's defiance and bald-faced flirting. If Dekker's endgame was to piss George off, he had achieved it.

George was spitting mad when he stomped down the sidewalk to Slade's Mercedes parked across the street. Slade got behind the wheel and started the engine. George got in and slammed the door shut. He buckled his seatbelt as Slade put the car in gear and pulled onto the road.

"What an asshole," George said. "That dickhead was hitting on you right in front of me."

Slade just shrugged. He had nothing to say. George was right. Dekker had been hitting on him in front of everyone. Now George was in the mood for a fight, but Slade wasn't going to rise to the bait. He simply didn't care anymore about what would or would not make George angry.

"Doesn't matter," George continued, mostly talking to himself now. "At the end of your little date it was me fucking your ass, and it was me who made you come."

That comment had Slade biting the inside of his cheek. He was about two seconds away from telling George that if it weren't for his own

71

sense of decency and honor, he would have fucked Dekker last night instead. Hell, he had almost caved and done just that. That same sense of decency and honor that had pushed Slade to call George the night before now kept Slade's mouth firmly shut. Slade pulled his sports car into a spot near George's front door and threw it in park, but he didn't turn the engine off.

"Aren't you coming in?" George asked as he unbuckled.

"No. I was being honest with Dekker. I have a lot to do before the show tonight," Slade answered. In one last attempt to let George show he was worth Slade's time and effort, Slade threw him a lifeline. He hoped George recognized it for what it was and grabbed on, because if he didn't, Slade was gone. For good. He ignored the voice in the back of his mind that was telling him he should already be gone. George's narcissism was so much more obvious to Slade now that he'd met Dekker.

"I have an extra invitation in the glove box. Come to the show tonight."

George looked at him. Slade knew a refusal was on the tip of his tongue, so he was surprised when George opened the glove box and removed the invitation without a word. He put the corner of the envelope to his forehead in a salute.

"See you tonight, babe," George said and opened the car door.

At the last second, he turned back to Slade, leaned over the console, and kissed him. It was long, slow, and gentle. George took his time with this one. It was so different from George's usual kisses and more like the ones they'd shared when they'd first started dating that Slade was speechless. He watched as George exited the car and headed into his apartment. Slade also didn't know exactly what to make of George's decision to attend the art show. That wasn't something he normally did. Slade hoped this was a sign that George was putting more effort into their relationship the second time around, but the reality was probably less noble. George was feeling threatened by Dekker so was making a point of one-upping the competition.

As Slade aimed the car toward Trendz, he wondered why he kept giving George chances to prove himself instead of running full speed toward Dekker. By the time he parked the car outside the art gallery, he had decided he was demented and enjoyed torturing himself. It was his only excuse for not diving headfirst into a relationship with Dekker when he knew it would be everything he fantasized about and exactly what he wanted.

☆☆☆

Dekker propped his head up with a hand under his chin as he scrolled through the wine list offered by The Cellar. Slade had been right about the variations. The appetizer menu had also been impressive. Even if the place hadn't belonged to the man Dekker was pursuing, he would have visited just for the food and wine. Dekker was always up for trying new things. A disclaimer at the bottom of the extensive menu stated the appetizers and wine selections were changed every few weeks. He'd already perused some of the art Slade displayed inside Trendz. None of it was traditional. Slade had told him he kept it modern and contemporary, but some of it was downright odd. Slade kept the artists and types of art exhibited on a regular rotation as well. Dekker smiled at Slade's ingenuity. Changing two or three things every so often was a great way to keep patrons coming back.

Dekker did something similar in his own store by changing out the outfits and adding new toys on a regular basis. Allowing a business to become stagnant was a great way to kill it. Always offer the customer fresh merchandise; that was Dekker's motto, and so far it had worked. People's expanding sexual appetites and attempts to bring back the romance also helped Callan's Closet stay in business. The population in general was becoming more adventurous and less close-minded about sex and sexuality.

Dekker leaned back in his office chair and scrubbed his palms over his face. He was tired. He'd been pulling a lot of long hours over the past two weeks after firing two employees for misconduct and theft. The pair had been caught after hours on the security tapes having sex on the front counter, wearing some of the costumes and using several products they'd taken off the shelves, all of which they had not paid for but had taken with them when they'd left.

It didn't help that Dekker was constantly thinking about Slade and how best to seduce the man. He hadn't seen Slade since the barbecue two weeks ago, but that hadn't dimmed his lust one bit. Dekker was more than ready for Slade to be the one helping him fall asleep at night instead of using his hand or the vibrating masturbation sleeve. Dekker smiled at the thought of slipping that sleeve over Slade's cock while Dekker rode his ass. One of the joys of owning a shop like his was that he had no shortage of ideas on how to keep Slade guessing and anticipating and deeply satisfied.

Dekker slid his hand down over his throbbing dick. The errant thought had him excited with no immediate outlet. He closed his eyes, pulled Slade's image up in his mind, and squeezed the thick shaft through his pants. A soft knock sounded on the office door, reminding him he was at work. Dekker sighed and straightened in his chair. He ran his hands through his hair as he yelled, "Come in."

Brad, Dekker's day-shift floor manager, stuck his head in. "There's a man here says he'd like to see you about a business opportunity. Gave me his card."

Brad walked into the office and handed Dekker a thick, black business card with the word Trendz embossed in gold Gothic lettering.

Dekker's heart rate kicked up, and he smiled, his fatigue completely forgotten. Slade was here.

"Send him back."

Brad nodded and disappeared through the door. When Slade appeared, Dekker was on his feet and in front of him before he was aware he had moved. Slade was wearing dark-gray slacks, a Goth-style blue button-down that highlighted the soft blue of his eyes, and a dark-blue silk tie. He'd fashioned his hair into disarrayed spikes. Dekker closed the office door and took Slade into his arms. Slade slipped his arms around Dekker's waist and squeezed.

"Damn, I've missed you. How've the past few weeks treated you?" Dekker asked as he pulled back to look Slade over without releasing him from the embrace. Dekker liked holding him too much to let go just yet. Slade seemed to feel the same way because he kept his hands on Dekker's hips.

"Pretty good actually. How about you?" Slade smiled, and Dekker went hot all over.

"Seeing you just made it great," Dekker said.

He already had a hard-on, and Slade's sexy voice and beautiful smile pushed Dekker to the edge of pain. Dekker leaned in and brushed a featherlight kiss over Slade's lips and then released the man. Not trusting himself completely, Dekker walked back to his chair, putting the desk between them, and pointed to the chair opposite. Slade watched intently as Dekker sat down before shaking himself out of whatever stupor he'd been in and took the seat Dekker had indicated. Dekker loved that the same simple kiss he bestowed on his friends could send Slade's brain into overdrive so easily. Dekker didn't even try to suppress his smile. Slade folded his hands in his lap and looked down.

"So did you come by just to see me, or do you really have business to discuss?" Dekker asked. He crossed his fingers, hoping the whole business thing was just a line so Slade could see him without raising suspicion.

"Honestly? A little of both," Slade answered with a shy smile. He looked up at Dekker through his lashes. Damn, that move was sexy, and Dekker adjusted himself under the desk. The slight blush on Slade's cheeks did funny things to Dekker's insides. Slade straightened up and ran a hand over his tie.

"So, I'm taking a risk on a new artist. She's pretty damn edgy with her artwork, but I think people need a little shock in their lives sometimes. She brought a few pieces to the gallery yesterday, and the first thing that popped into my head while I was looking them over was your store."

"My store?" Dekker asked. He braced his weight on his forearms as he leaned over the desk and smiled suggestively. "Or me?"

Slade chuckled. "What's the difference? Both are sex driven."

Dekker's smile widened, and he laughed a bit. "True, for the moment. I'm a little obsessed with getting you naked and burying myself inside you."

Slade blushed furiously and closed his eyes. "You're gonna be the death of me," he whispered. He opened his eyes and leveled his blue gaze on Dekker. "Anyway, this artist does a lot of nude, bondage, sexually based themes. She doesn't shy away from same-sex or interracial pairings, either. The last time I was here I remembered that other than the product lining the shelves there's no real decoration, and I see that hasn't changed." Slade scooted his chair closer to the desk and leaned onto it, mimicking Dekker's position. His excitement over the subject was almost palpable.

"So I was thinking we could both make bank off her. If you're willing, I could post an ad for the art show at Trendz with brochures and business cards at your front door and hang a few of her art pieces around the store. Instead of making it an invite-only kind of art show, I would make it a revolving-door party where people could pay a cover charge at the door and come and go as they please. What do you think?"

Dekker smiled at Slade's obvious enthusiasm over the idea. "I think that's a great idea, and I will absolutely let you advertise here. Not sure how it helps my business, but I'll do anything for you if you keep looking at me with that sparkle in your eyes and talking because damn, baby, your voice is sexy as hell."

Slade's eyes drifted to Dekker's mouth, and he leaned forward slightly. Dekker's smile slipped a bit as he prepared for Slade to kiss him. He knew Slade's kiss would rock his world now the same way it had the night of their date, but it didn't happen. Slade caught himself. Slade slapped his palms on the desk and pushed back in his seat. Both men licked their lips and swallowed hard.

"Sorry, um, I got a little...carried away. The kind of people who will be attending this type of art show are going to be more, shall we say, liberal, than my usual patrons," Slade said.

"Yeah, I would say so," Dekker agreed.

"I thought it would add to the fun and the theme of the artwork if you set up a table in the back of the gallery selling your products."

Dekker leaned back in his seat as Slade's business proposal started rolling through his brain. "So the idea you have is to tantalize their sex drive with artwork of nude people tied up and then offer them a way to live that fantasy by buying the restraints from me?"

"Exactly," Slade said with a nod. "The artist is bringing everything she wants to have in the show to the gallery tomorrow. If this is something you want to do, I think you should be there. That way you can bring the sex toys and outfits that best fit with the images I'll be displaying."

"Anything that allows me to spend time with you," Dekker said. He knew he was coming on strong, but damn it, he wanted Slade. And he wanted Slade to know it.

"I'm still with George," Slade said softly.

Dekker shrugged. He'd had a feeling George might still be in the picture since Slade hadn't contacted him, but he didn't care.

"And you're with Alek."

That comment hit Dekker like a train, stopping all thought processes. "What?" he asked in shock. Where the hell had Slade gotten the idea he and Alek were a couple? Dekker ran his hands through his hair and creased his brow. "Where the hell did that come from?"

"Just...things I've seen and heard..." Slade started, but Dekker cut him off with a slash of his hand.

"Do you honestly think I would be coming onto you the way I am if I was seeing someone else?" Dekker asked. He couldn't believe where this conversation was suddenly going. He was also angry, the implication that he would cheat not going unnoticed. "What the hell kind of man do you think I am?" he snapped and rose to his feet.

"*My* being taken hasn't stopped you," Slade said as he too stood up.

"No, Slade. No," Dekker said angrily as he came around the desk to square off with Slade. "That's not the same thing, and you know it. If I were taken, I would lust after you in silence and maybe question why I was hot for someone other than my boyfriend, but I would never act on it. Never. I don't cheat."

"Neither do I, Dekker, but you sure don't have a problem trying to make me," Slade nearly shouted.

Dekker cupped Slade's face, and Slade latched onto Dekker's wrists. Dekker kept his voice low and steady. "I'm not trying to make you cheat on him. I'm trying to make you leave him."

Slade's grip tightened, and Dekker released him. It was either that or kiss him. Dekker backed several feet away. He had so much more to say, but no idea how to go about it. Too many words jostled for attention in his brain, all of them wanting to be said first.

"This was a bad idea," Slade said softly.

"No, it was a great idea. You have a good head for business. You have my card, email me the details for tomorrow's meeting, and I'll be there. And I promise to keep it professional."

☆☆☆

Slade paced across his office, trying to slow his breathing and calm his nerves. He was on the verge of a panic attack. Dekker had been true to his word, keeping every interaction between them the past two weeks on a professional level. And fuck if that didn't just make Dekker all the more irresistible. They had spent several hours discussing the upcoming show over the past four days, making changes, solidifying plans. Now, the night was here, and Slade was a wreck.

Dekker and one of his employees, Dixie, were setting up the Callan's Closet table along the back wall of the gallery. Slade's bartender, Jose, was getting The Cellar ready, and two waitresses, Sandy and Corinne, were placing appetizers on trays and tables strategically placed in both the restaurant and the art gallery. Having Dekker around when his relationship with George had once again become rocky was unnerving.

Over the past week, Slade had become increasingly suspicious over his inability to reach George on the phone. It had been one of the warning signs Slade had ignored the first time around when George was cheating, so it was one of the things Slade was watching closely now. Squaring his shoulders, Slade slid his professionalism back in place as he opened the office door. He stepped into the hall only to be brought up short by a mass of impeccably dressed male.

"Sorry," Dekker said and stepped back several inches. "Just checking to make sure you're okay. You seem off tonight."

"I know. I'm all over the map emotionally," Slade admitted. He just could not lie to this man.

"I can understand. This show is risky and risqué, especially with Callan's Closet here," Dekker said and slid his hands into his pockets. "But hey, relax. They say all press is good press, right?"

Dekker smiled and returned to his table to help Dixie lay out the remaining items. Slade's gaze moved over the assortment of products Dekker had brought to sell and nodded. This was going to be one hell of a show. He just hoped it was lucrative for both of them. Slade had previously hosted a few shows he'd had high expectations for that had failed miserably. He'd learned long ago it was difficult to pinpoint people's tastes and the turn of fads. It was what had led him to buy The Cellar and offer more than just art. Even if none of the artwork sold, he still made money off the wine and food.

Slade discreetly looked Dekker over. The man cleaned up well. Slade thought he was delicious in jeans and a T-shirt. Dressed in a suit and tie, with his shoulder-length hair pulled into a ponytail at the nape of his neck, the man was incredibly hot. Dekker would make a killing off vibrators alone if the women attending tonight were half as hot and bothered by him as Slade was. Dekker had once complimented Slade's head for business, but Slade knew Dekker had good business sense, too. He had brought Dixie, a stacked bombshell of black-haired beauty dressed in a tight, red sheath of a dress that showed plenty of skin, topped off with fuck-me heels to appeal to the male attendees. Slade wondered if the artwork would get any attention at all with Dekker and Dixie present.

Slade made one more pass through the gallery, making sure everything was lit properly and displayed in the best way possible. He passed by the bar and buffet tables, pleased to see his employees had done remarkably well at preparing the food and drinks. They had never let him down before and tonight would be no exception. Pleased that everything was ready, he collected Raven, the artist, and opened the doors to greet guests. After the first dozen or so people had entered, Slade's nerves disappeared, and the night became business as usual. The next six hours flew by in a flurry of activity that felt like home to Slade. He loved the energy and excitement, and the crowd tonight was wired more intensely than usual. At midnight, he closed and locked the door behind the last customer.

"Nicely done, people," Slade said with a huge smile.

Everyone whooped and clapped, congratulating Raven on her successful art show, and then dispersed to their designated areas to start cleaning up. Slade caught Dekker's smile as he and Dixie made their way to the back of the gallery to take down their display. As he passed, Slade hugged Raven and kissed her cheek. They had sold around half the pieces she'd brought, making her first show a huge success. She was a bubbly, happy mess, and he sent her home with the reminder to come back tomorrow afternoon to collect her profit and finalize the contract. On his way to the office, Slade stopped by Dekker's table.

"How did it go for you tonight?" he asked. Dixie gave him a thumbs-up and disappeared into the bathroom with a change of clothes. As Dekker turned those hazel eyes on him, his breath hitched. Dekker's smile was blinding.

"We sold out. For the last half hour, I was handing out cards with ten percent off any item in the store written on them as IOU's."

"Damn," Slade breathed. He hadn't expected that, and it was clear that Dekker hadn't either.

"I know, right? Fucking fine advertisement if you ask me. Lots of horny people out there."

"Well, I'm sure you and Dixie had something to do with that. The two of you looked sexy as hell, and surrounded by naughty toys? Fuck. I imagine you fueled quite a few fantasies tonight," Slade said and watched as Dekker's eyes darkened with desire before Dekker turned away. Dekker had certainly given Slade plenty of ideas that would be front and center for the foreseeable future. The phone in Slade's office rang, and he excused himself to answer it.

"Trendz Art Gallery," he said into the receiver.

"It's me," George said softly. "I think I left my damn wallet there this morning. Do you see it?"

Slade glanced around the immediate area. "No. Do you think it's in the office here, or could it be anywhere in the gallery? I just finished a show, and no one said anything about finding a wallet."

"Damn. I thought I put it on the desk in your office," George whispered.

"No. I don't see it. Why are you whispering?"

"Is it on the file cabinet?" George asked, ignoring Slade's question completely and making Slade uncomfortable.

"No, George, your wallet isn't here. What the hell is going on? Why are you being so quiet?"

"I can't find my fucking wallet, that's what's going on," George hissed into the phone.

"Your wallet's on the kitchen table, baby," said an unfamiliar male voice on the other end of the phone, and Slade closed his eyes. Anger and betrayal blasted through his system. Unlike the voice of the man with George, the emotions were all too familiar.

"You motherfucker," Slade whispered. His legs became weak, and he half sat, half fell into the chair behind his desk.

"Slade..." George started, but Slade hung up on him. He didn't need or want to hear George's excuses. He'd heard them all the first time around. Slade rested his elbows on the desk and buried his face in his hands. There were no tears this time, no pain, just anger that was mostly directed at himself. Why he had believed George could change and keep his dick in his pants, Slade didn't know.

"Hey, Slade, where do you want me to put these tables?"

Slade lifted his head in surprise as Dekker stepped into his office. He hadn't realized he'd left the door open. Dekker's face fell as he looked at Slade slumped over the desk.

"Are you okay?" Dekker asked.

"Uh, I don't know yet. Ask me again later. You can put the tables in the storage area around back," Slade said and rose to his feet as the phone started ringing again.

Dekker glanced at the ringing phone, noted Slade's refusal to answer it, then nodded and left the room. Slade once again put his professional face on and stepped back out onto the floor to help clean and close. Corinne, Sandy, and Jose finished up in the restaurant and walked out to their cars with Dixie. Dekker had excused himself to use the restroom while Slade closed down the restaurant and locked the office. Slade shut down the lights as he made his way to the front of the gallery and found Dekker waiting for him by the door.

Dekker had undone his tie, but left it hanging around his neck, and opened the top few buttons of his shirt, giving Slade a peek of fine chest hair. Slade knew Dekker had done it for comfort and was completely unaware that the sight sent Slade's mind and body into sexual overload. Unfortunately, the realization that George had once again cheated on him was still too fresh, and Slade felt too tired and stupid to do anything more than go home.

"It's later," Dekker said as Slade joined him at the door.

"Huh?" Slade asked absently as he set the alarm. He pushed Dekker out ahead of him and closed the door. He waited until he heard the security alarm engage and then headed for the parking lot. He was vaguely aware of Dekker following close behind.

"You told me to ask later if you were okay. It's later," Dekker said.

Slade stopped and stared down the street without really seeing anything. "Yeah, I'm fine. I'm a fucking idiot for taking that lying bastard back, but I'm fine."

Slade was suddenly surrounded by Dekker's heat as Dekker wrapped strong arms around him. Dekker pulled him back against his chest and held him tightly. The embrace was comforting and supportive rather than sexual like their previous encounters had been. It was exactly what Slade needed, and it made perfect sense that Dekker would be the one giving it.

"Can I call you later?" Dekker asked softly.

"Yes," Slade answered immediately.

Dekker squeezed Slade quickly and then released him. Dekker smiled at him as he walked down the street to his truck. Slade stood on the sidewalk and listened as the truck's engine roared to life and then watched Dekker disappear into the night. As Slade approached his car in the parking lot at the side of the building, the screech of tires had him turning around in alarm. George's sedan came to a halt at an angle a few spaces away. George left the car running as he got out and stomped to where Slade stood by his Mercedes. Slade backed away until his back pressed against the car. He'd never seen George this angry before.

George shoved Slade against the car, grabbed his face, and took Slade's mouth in a bruising kiss. Slade put his palms to George's chest in an attempt to push him away, but he couldn't get enough leverage. George fisted Slade's hair to hold him in place as he forced his tongue into Slade's mouth. He rolled his hips forward, pressing his erection into Slade's hip. He broke the kiss, but he kept Slade's hair in his fist and their bodies pressed together.

"You feel that?" George asked as he pumped his hips forward again. "Feel that fucking cock? It's for you," he bit out angrily.

"Hell it is. You've probably shoved that thing into every available ass in town," Slade said, just as angrily.

George's eyes narrowed, and his fist tightened in Slade's hair. He pulled back, taking Slade with him, then violently spun Slade around and slammed his chest into the car. George pushed against him from behind and pulled his head back by his hair. George slid his hand between Slade's body and the car and then continued down the front of Slade's pants. He palmed Slade's dick and squeezed as he pumped his pelvis into Slade's ass. The deep rumble of an engine drew closer, and just as Slade got his hands against the car in a position that allowed him leverage to push George off him, headlights illuminated them. George leapt away from him, and Slade turned around to see Dekker get out of his truck.

"Oh, I get it now you little shit. You can fuck him behind my back, but God forbid I have a little action on the side," George yelled.

"Bullshit. I never cheated on you with anyone," Slade said.

"Yeah, right. That whole charity date thing was a lie so you could go fuck him without me being suspicious. I'll bet you had quite the little orgy in the office at that barbecue, too. He bend you over the desk and fuck you while you sucked the biker's dick? I saw the camera. Got your spunk-covered face on tape?"

"Shut up, George. You're sick. You know that? God, what was I thinking dating you?" Slade asked no one in particular. "Just leave. Go home or wherever the hell you were when you called, but don't ever come near me again."

"This isn't over," George said as he walked back to his car.

"Yes, it is," Slade said loudly as George closed the door and turned his car around. Slade watched as George drove out of the lot and disappeared. He turned his attention to Dekker, who stood next to his truck with his arms crossed. "What are you doing here?" Slade hadn't meant to snap at Dekker, but his anger was bristling and overflowing. He had little control right now.

"I realized I'd left you out here alone in the middle of the night. I turned around to make sure you got to your car safely," Dekker answered. His voice was calm, low, and steady. "I'll stay until you're in your car."

Dekker opened his truck door and climbed behind the wheel. Slade felt like shit. It was bad enough that his relationship with George had dissolved into a physical confrontation, but it was made worse by the fact that Dekker had witnessed it. He felt about two seconds away from internally combusting. Slade couldn't remember if he'd unlocked the car before George had pulled up, so he pushed the button on the key fob to make sure the doors were locked. When the horn honked, indicating the alarm was set, Slade turned around to walk to Dekker's truck. As he approached the passenger door, he heard the snick of the lock opening. Slade climbed into the warmth of the truck's cab and put his seat belt on.

"I need to go out," Slade said without looking at Dekker.

Dekker put the truck in drive and pulled out. "I know just the thing," he said.

The drive was passed in silence, and Slade was grateful Dekker didn't push for answers or force him to talk about nonsense. While Slade's thoughts were roiling, silence was preferable. He looked out the windshield blindly, only becoming aware of his surroundings when Dekker put the truck in park and turned off the engine. Slade looked at the building in front of them.

"Laser tag?" Slade asked.

"The only way to legally shoot people in the head," Dekker said with a smile. "And it's a whole lot of fun."

Chapter Ten

Dekker held Slade's hand as they entered the arcade and walked to the back where the laser tag was located. At one a.m. the clientele was mostly twenty-somethings with alcohol on board. It was noisy and chaotic and perfect for Slade to unleash whatever emotions were plaguing him. It was also perfect for Dekker. He had a few pent-up emotions of his own. White-hot rage had lanced through his chest when he'd pulled into the parking lot and seen George holding Slade against the car. He didn't even want to think about where that encounter might have led if he hadn't shown up. They walked up to the counter, and Dekker reached for his wallet only to have his hand slapped away.

"Oh, hell no," Slade said. "You said I could pay the next time, and this is the next time."

Slade pulled his own wallet out and paid for two games for each of them. They were given buzzers that would alert them when their turn came up, which the attendant told them would only be about ten minutes. Dekker threaded his fingers through Slade's again and led him toward a secluded table in the corner. Slade squeezed his hand and then pulled away toward the bar. He came back a few minutes later with two whiskeys on ice. They sat in silence, watching those around them and letting the whiskey calm their nerves. The buzzer vibrated across the table, and Dekker snapped it up. They polished off their drinks in one big gulp and headed toward the laser tag air lock. Once they were suited up and the rules had been given, the attendant moved to the door and opened it. Dekker and Slade followed behind six others into the darkened room on the other side. Slade pushed up against Dekker's body and leaned in close to his ear.

"I'm going to hunt you down and nail your ass," he whispered with a twinkle in his eye.

Dekker smiled at him, the double entendre received loud and clear. He blew Slade a kiss and then took off around a corner. And the game was on. Because of the low number of people wanting to play, their two twenty-minute games were back-to-back. Toward the middle of the second round, Slade grabbed him from behind and used him as a human shield against another player. Dekker laughed as Slade maneuvered him back and forth, popping out and shooting the others from around his body at random intervals. Dekker had long since lost his pack life, having taken too many hits, and just let Slade have his fun.

After a few minutes, the opponent's attention was drawn by his girlfriend who started shooting at him from the second level. Slade pulled Dekker around a corner, slammed his back against the wall, and jumped him. The laser tag vests made it awkward as hell to get close, but Slade did his best. His hot lips and tongue feasted on Dekker's mouth like the world would end when the sun rose. Dekker held Slade's hips lightly and simply enjoyed the fact that Slade was taking control.

The horn sounded, signaling the end of the game, and the house lights came on. Slade pushed away and wound his way through the maze to the door, Dekker close behind. They replaced their vests and gun packs on the hooks and returned to the arcade. Both men were grinning broadly and once again holding hands as they left the building. Dekker glanced down at his watch. It was just after two a.m. on a Saturday night. His body was telling him he was exhausted, but his mind was wide awake. Slade pulled him to a stop at the truck.

"I know after the way I was kissing you this will sound odd, but can you sleep with me and not have sex?" he asked.

"Yes, if that's what you want," Dekker answered.

"I don't know what I want. I mean, I know I want you, but I'm so messed up right now that I can't...I don't want you to feel like you're my rebound."

Dekker squeezed Slade's hand and brought it to his lips. He brushed his lips lightly over the knuckles and smiled. "Get in the truck, and tell me where I'm driving."

Chapter Eleven

Slade got in the truck and decided there was really only one option. He would be spending the night at Dekker's place because he was worried about George lying in wait at his apartment and because his roommate, Phil, was probably home. Dekker brought the truck's engine to life with a rumble and looked at Slade, the question of "Where to?" burning in his eyes.

"I have a roommate," Slade said.

"Fuck yes. My place it is," Dekker breathed as he pulled out of the lot.

Slade admired the houses they passed when Dekker pulled off the main roads and onto neighborhood streets. He parked the truck in the driveway of a nice ranch-style house with an attached garage. As Dekker led the way to the door, Slade looked around at the houses nearby. Most of the driveways were empty; the cars tucked safely in the garages.

"Truck too big for the garage?" Slade asked with a smile. Dekker shook his head and smiled back. "Oh, damn. You're not overcompensating are you? Big truck, small dick?"

Dekker barked out a laugh. "Uh, no, handsome. Nothing small on me. My baby is in the garage."

Dekker held the front door open and ushered Slade in first. Slade moved past him, making sure he rubbed up against Dekker's body in the process. "Your baby?"

"My Ducati." Dekker closed the door.

"Big truck and fast motorcycle. You are overcompensating," Slade said, though his smile never wavered.

"Well, I haven't had a boyfriend in a long damn time and haven't had sex in...whew, six months or so. Got to get my thrills somewhere."

"Ah, the sex shop makes so much sense now. Sex for one has never been more fun," Slade said as he followed Dekker down the hall to the bedroom.

"Shit, man, that's good. I'm gonna use that in a print ad or something." Dekker pulled Slade into his arms. He walked backward toward the bed, taking Slade with him. "Do you know how long I've wanted you?" Dekker asked. Slade held his gaze and shook his head. "Since I heard that sexy-as-fuck voice of yours at the fundraiser."

"I got a couple hours on you, then. I've wanted you since I first saw you walk on stage in those leather pants and that vest. I could barely breathe. Those pants left little to the imagination," Slade said as he reached down to cup Dekker's crotch. Dekker grabbed Slade around the wrist and gently pulled his hand up, placing Slade's palm to his chest.

"If you want sleep with no sex, don't touch there," Dekker said softly.

Slade groaned and dropped his head on Dekker's shoulder.

"We've both had a long night, and we're exhausted. Do what you got to do and get in bed. Bathroom's there."

Dekker spun Slade and pushed him in the direction of the en-suite bathroom while he headed into the guest bath down the hall. Slade stripped to his boxers, brushed his teeth with a new toothbrush he found in the cabinet, and splashed water on his face. By the time he exited the bathroom, Dekker was in bed with the lights out. Slade mapped out a route to the bed and then shut off the light and plunged the room into darkness. Slade shuffled his way to the bed until his knees bumped the mattress. It dipped under his weight as he climbed under the blankets and scooted against Dekker's hot body. After a few minutes of adjustments, minor injuries, and childish, fatigue-induced giggling, they finally got comfortable with Dekker spooning Slade, his arms wrapped tightly around him. Slade was enveloped in Dekker's scent and heat. He'd never been more comfortable and relaxed.

Dekker took a deep breath and exhaled slowly. "Finally," he whispered and tugged Slade closer. "I've got you right where I want you, right where you belong." He kissed Slade behind the ear, and Slade closed his eyes.

Chapter Twelve

A ringing phone dragged Dekker out of a dream he was rather enjoying and into the harsh reality of sun blazing through the curtains. He answered with a gruff hello while rubbing the remnants of sleep from his eyes.

"So, how was your night?" Alek asked.

"Rudely interrupted by you," Dekker answered.

"It's ten a.m., Dek. How's Slade this morning?"

"I don't know. I haven't seen him." Dekker sat up and swung his legs over the side of the bed. He needed to pee, and since it didn't sound like Alek was going to keep this conversation short, he made his way into the bathroom, put the phone on speaker, and set it on the sink.

"Okay, you're tired and grumpy, so let me get right to it," Alek said.

"That would be awesome," Dekker said as he took care of business.

"First, I can't believe you're taking a piss while on the phone with me! Seriously, dude. Second, I had a very interesting call at seven this morning. Want to know from whom?"

Dekker washed his hands, then swiped the phone off the sink, and put it to his ear. He had just woken up and felt that irritability finely honed by fatigue poking at him. He needed caffeine and about eight more hours of sleep. He padded down the hall in his boxers and bare feet toward the kitchen.

"I don't really care," Dekker told Alek.

"Slade's roommate, Phil. Apparently, he was woken up around one a.m. because George was pounding on the door, screaming at Slade to open up. Kind of concerned Phil because Slade wasn't there. George told him about you showing up, and when Slade didn't come home, Phil called me. Now I'm a bit concerned because Slade was last seen with you, but you're saying you haven't seen him..."

Alek's rant was cut off when Dekker entered the kitchen and yelped, jumping in surprise. The phone slipped from his hand. He tried to catch it unsuccessfully, jostling it all the way to the floor. Slade's deep laughter filled the room as Dekker snatched his phone off the hardwood floor.

"Talk to Alek before he sends out cadaver dogs or something," Dekker said as he shoved the phone at Slade.

Dekker let Slade's husky voice roll over him without really listening to the words. Right now all he cared about was getting some coffee in him. It was a sad commentary on Dekker's love life that when he woke up alone he would assume Slade had gone home. The last thing he had expected, though secretly hoped for, was to find Slade sitting at his kitchen table. He was drinking coffee and reading something on his cell phone while wearing nothing but his dress pants from the night before.

Three of Dekker's senses were getting slammed to the ground right now: the sight of Slade half dressed, the man's incredible scent, and the sound of his sexy voice as he spoke to Alek. Dekker's cock was straining inside his boxers. He sipped his own steaming brew and turned around to face Slade. He leaned back against the counter and crossed one foot over the other. He knew the moment Slade saw the bulge because he blushed slightly and swallowed hard. Slade disconnected the call and slowly looked up, taking in every inch of Dekker's bare skin. He handed the phone back with a smile and Dekker took it, giving Slade a flirty wink.

"You forgot I came home with you last night, didn't you?" Slade asked. His face looked amused, but Dekker thought he heard a little hurt lacing those words.

"No. I remember every second of last night. But you weren't in bed when Alek called, so I assumed you'd gone home," Dekker admitted.

"Is that what you wanted?" Slade's smile thinned a bit.

"Yes, Slade, I've pined over you for almost two months, finally got you in bed with me, and wanted you gone by morning." Dekker sipped his coffee.

Slade rolled his eyes as he rose to his feet. He closed the distance between them, pressed their bare chests together, and rested his hands on Dekker's hips.

"Such a smart ass," Slade said softly and nibbled at Dekker's stubble-covered jaw. He flicked his tongue out over the morning growth, and Dekker shuddered, gooseflesh exploding across his entire body. That one sexy move had all Dekker's nerve endings firing at once.

"I have a shirt that says 'I Speak Fluent Sarcastic,'" Dekker said.

He closed his eyes and moaned with embarrassment. Slade was being sexy, pushing Dekker's arousal into the stratosphere, and he went and said something idiotic. He felt ten shades of stupid, but Slade just laughed and moved his lips across Dekker's jaw to his earlobe. When Slade sucked the sensitive skin into his mouth, Dekker thumped his coffee mug on the granite, ignoring the fact that some spilled, and gripped the edge of the counter as his knees went weak.

Dekker lowered his head to give Slade's neck the same treatment. He was rewarded with Slade pressing their bodies tighter together and fisting Dekker's long, sleep-disheveled hair. Dekker risked falling to the ground by releasing his grip on the counter and wrapping his arms around Slade's waist, holding the man he wanted more than his next breath close to him. Slade pulled his head away, gently tugging Dekker back by his hair so they could look into each other's eyes.

"Do you think it's possible George was his own rebound?" Slade asked.

Dekker cleared his throat and blinked rapidly to clear his lust-addled brain. Those incredible blue eyes and that husky voice were mesmerizing. "It might be the blood rushing south, but that question doesn't make sense to me," he answered.

Slade chuckled. "George and I were together about eight months when he cheated on me, and I kicked him to the curb. We were separated for three weeks before I took his lying ass back. When we got back together, it was like...I didn't get involved. You know what I mean? The emotion was gone, so when I dumped his ass again last night, I didn't feel anything, except stupid for setting myself up for the same damn thing as before. Fool me twice, shame on me. I'm rambling again, but my point is the relationship was physical and nothing more, so maybe he wasn't just an old boyfriend, maybe he was the rebound boyfriend, too."

How Slade managed to get that all out in only two breaths, Dekker couldn't fathom. He also couldn't think straight. Slade's cock was pulsing against his own, making it nearly impossible to hold any kind of thought in his head that didn't center on fucking Slade into the mattress.

"Um, sure. Why are we talking about George?" Dekker asked, trying to pull his scattered brain cells together long enough to get through this conversation.

"I'm trying to have sex with you, Dekker." The smile Slade gifted him had his poor, neglected cock leaking. "I just can't handle the idea of you being a rebound to fucking George."

"No. No fucking George. Fuck me," Dekker said and kissed Slade's laughing mouth.

Slade pulled away and grabbed one of Dekker's hands to lead him back down the hall to the bedroom. Dekker's eyes were riveted by the movement of Slade's butt and thigh muscles beneath his tailored slacks as he walked. His mouth went dry. He couldn't wait to get those pants off and slide between those perfect round cheeks.

☆☆☆

"Do you top or bottom?" Slade asked as he turned around in the bedroom to face Dekker, pulling him into his arms. One of Dekker's hands cupped Slade's ass while he used the other to toy with Slade's nipple.

"Hmm?" was Dekker's distracted response. Slade laughed outright and peppered Dekker's jaw with tiny love bites. Slade took advantage of Dekker's lack of attention to whisper, "I'm falling for you."

Slade's gut twisted up once he uttered the words. He knew Dekker wanted him. The man had never kept that secret, but Slade wondered if making his feelings known to Dekker so soon was the smartest thing to do. Slade relaxed when it appeared Dekker hadn't heard his heartfelt words. Slade separated their bodies and cupped Dekker's face, forcing the beautiful man to look him in the eye. When he had Dekker's full attention, he asked, "What do you want, you drop-dead gorgeous man?"

"You," Dekker answered.

Slade was exceptionally amused that Dekker went stupid with lust, and he loved that he was the one who had pushed Dekker to this point. Sex was going to be interesting if Slade had to pick up the lead. That wasn't normal for him. Slade was once again taken by surprise when Dekker spun him around and pulled him back against his chest. Dekker held him with an arm around his waist and a hand pressed to his chest.

"Damn, I can't decide how I want you first. I've imagined you bent over every piece of furniture or on your back spread open for me in every room of this house for the past two months," Dekker said, voice rough with desire. He held Slade tightly as Slade dropped his hands to his pants, opened them, and let them fall to the floor, revealing his tented boxers beneath. Dekker slowly walked Slade to the bed. "I've also imagined the roles were reversed, and it was me bent over or spread out for you," Dekker whispered. "How do you want our first time to be, Slade?"

Slade had told Dekker he was falling for him, but those words cinched the deal. Slade was completely and hopelessly in love with Dekker Callan. Even at a time like this, when Dekker seemed so aloof and sex-driven, he was thinking of Slade and what Slade wanted. Right this moment, Slade would give Dekker whatever he wanted. Not because he felt he had to, but because he wanted to.

"I want you just like this." Slade reached behind him to grab hold of Dekker's ass. He squeezed the taut muscles and was rewarded with Dekker's low groan of pleasure. "I want you naked, behind me, holding me against you while you fuck—"

Dekker's hand slapped down over Slade's mouth, cutting off his words. "Those words in that voice will have me blowing my load before I even get my shorts off. Shhh," Dekker said softly in Slade's ear.

Slade bit his bottom lip and looked over his shoulder at Dekker as they separated just enough to remove their underwear. Anxiety and excitement fought for dominance in Slade's chest as they both got their first look at each other's bodies. Magnificent was the only word Slade could think of to describe Dekker naked, his muscles toned, but not bulging, and a light dusting of hair surrounding the biggest cock Slade had had the pleasure of seeing.

"You're right," Slade said, slowly raising his eyes to meet Dekker's gaze. He smiled at the confusion sparring with sexual hunger in those hazel orbs. "Nothing small on you."

The humor that instantly sparked to life on Dekker's face was beautiful. Dekker waggled his eyebrows as he moved back into Slade's space and kissed him. Despite the crazed sexual energy they were both feeling, Dekker kept the kiss soft and slow, gradually deepening it until their tongues were dancing, bodies pressed so close their cocks were sliding along one another, and neither man could wait any longer for release.

Slade let go of Dekker's hair and turned in his arms, only breaking the kiss when his shoulder brushing across Dekker's chest pushed him out of reach. With Dekker's hard shaft rubbing along the cleft of his ass, Slade's need for the man to be inside him reached an all-time high. He moved onto the bed with Dekker following, Dekker's hold loosening but not releasing. Slade kept his legs together because he had no choice the way Dekker straddled him, pinning his legs between Dekker's knees. Dekker used his body weight to press Slade down to his stomach on the mattress.

Slade lay there surrounded by Dekker's heat and strength and wondered why he'd waited so long for this. He once again berated himself for not telling George to take a hike when he'd asked Slade to give him a second chance. Slade had already set eyes on Dekker at that point. He had known then he had the hots for the man. And he certainly should have told George it wasn't going to happen after the first date when he realized Dekker was the man of his dreams.

His train of thought derailed when Dekker lifted off him. Slade's head came off the mattress in alarm before Dekker kissed the indentation above his butt crack, his long soft hair and morning stubble tickling over sensitive skin at the base of his spine.

Slade tipped his ass up and spread his legs to offer Dekker access. Dekker kissed, bit, and licked over Slade's lower back, butt cheeks, and thighs, working him up higher and higher until he was begging for Dekker to fill him. Dekker shushed him again gently and then slicked two fingers in his mouth. Slade rested his head on the blanket and tried to relax for the invasion he knew was coming. As strung out as he was feeling, he hoped he wouldn't blow the second Dekker slid a finger in.

That would be beyond embarrassing. He felt Dekker's fingers press against his pucker and forced himself to relax and accept what Dekker gave. Slade lifted his hips and moaned at the burn of Dekker's slow push. Dekker kissed and massaged Slade's straining muscles until Slade relaxed around him, and he was sliding his fingers in and out with ease.

"More, Dekker, please," Slade said as he pushed back on Dekker's digits. He thought he was going to get what he'd asked for when Dekker pulled his fingers out. Slade heard the pop and squirt of a lube bottle, but nearly cried in desperation when Dekker slid three lubed fingers inside him instead of a lubed cock.

"Dekker, please just fuck me," Slade begged.

"I need to open you, get you ready," Dekker said softly and then leaned over Slade's body to kiss him between the shoulder blades. "I won't hurt you." Breath from the words ghosted over Slade's spine, making him shiver.

"You won't. I want to feel the burn of you stretching me. God, it makes me hot just thinking about you pushing inside. I want to come with you buried balls deep…"

Dekker's pained moan cut Slade short. He tried not to whimper at the emptiness he felt when Dekker pulled his fingers free. He knew what was about to replace them would be far more filling—and fulfilling. Slade closed his eyes and waited with barely contained anticipation as the erotic sounds of Dekker tearing open a condom and rolling it down his thick shaft teased his ears. Dekker pushed Slade's legs open a little wider, settling his shins over the back of Slade's knees. Dekker slid a hand under Slade's arm and gripped his shoulder as he used his other hand to guide the tip of his penis into Slade's ass. Slade gasped as the initial pain lanced through him when the mushroom head popped in.

Dekker held still, rubbing Slade's body shoulder to hip, as Slade fought to adjust to the large intrusion, and Dekker fought off his orgasm. Just the tip was in, and he was ready to shoot from Slade's tight, silken heat. Dekker thrust his hips once and slid in a little farther.

"No," Slade said, and Dekker froze. "One slow push in. I want to feel every inch of that monster stretching me."

Dekker pressed his knees into the bed, allowing his legs to drape over Slade's calves, lowered his chest to Slade's back to rest his elbow beside Slade's head, and slid his fingers through Slade's hair. He slowly moved his body up Slade's back and felt his cock move deeper into Slade's ass. Slade's moan escalated into a shouted "Fuck yes" as Dekker sank all the way, scrotum high and tight against Slade's perineum. Slade reached up and threaded his fingers through Dekker's hair, pulling him down so he could kiss his cheek and jaw, tonguing the stubble covering his skin. Dekker buried his face in Slade's neck and began pumping his hips at a pace he thought he could maintain. With every thrust of his hips, he pushed Slade's pelvis down into the mattress, hoping the friction would bring Slade to orgasm as quickly as Slade's tight, silky channel convulsing around his cock was bringing him to orgasm. He gritted his teeth against the need to come.

"Slade," he bit out. "Come with me."

Slade adjusted his body beneath Dekker, causing Dekker to stop thrusting. Slade pulled Dekker's hand from his shoulder and guided it down to his cock. Dekker wrapped his fingers around Slade's pulsing shaft, Slade's hand over his. Slade squeezed and released their joined fingers over his dick as Dekker slammed into his ass with unrelenting force. It was a frantic pounding to the finish line, and Dekker crossed it first. His thrusts stuttered, and his breathing hitched in an attempt to hold off, to wait for Slade, but in the end his orgasm blasted out of him, filling the condom.

☆☆☆

Slade felt Dekker's movements falter and knew he was coming. He clenched his ass around the cock inside him. Dekker kissed his neck and rolled to his side, pulling Slade with him. He moved his hand over Slade's throbbing dick with purpose. Slade grabbed the arm across his chest with one hand and held on as he helped Dekker work him up to a mind-blowing orgasm. Slade shouted as he came; his thick, hot semen coated the bedspread and their joined hands. Dekker released Slade's softening cock and threaded their slick fingers together. He pulled his hips back far enough to pull free of Slade's ass and then immediately pressed his body against Slade's back. Dekker held him in a tight embrace for several long minutes, peppering his neck and shoulder with kisses while Slade lay in his arms in a boneless, satisfied heap.

"You okay?" Dekker asked between kisses.

Slade smiled lazily. "Perfect."

Slade twisted in Dekker's arms. Their mouths came together in a sensual press of lips, opening occasionally to allow entry to a questing tongue. The kiss was slow, loving, and tender without losing an ounce of its sexual heat.

"Slade," Dekker said when Slade broke the kiss to get more comfortable. Slade had been moving to kiss Dekker again but stopped with their lips barely brushing together. He looked into Dekker's eyes.

"I'm falling for you, too."

Slade's heart stuttered, and his face went hot. He averted his eyes to Dekker's stubble-covered chin. "I didn't think you heard."

"I heard." Dekker kissed Slade on the forehead and then started to untangle their limbs. "We're going to be permanently stuck together if we don't wash up."

"I can think of worse things," Slade said.

Dekker slid off the side of the bed and turned to see Slade still lying on his back across the mattress, smiling broadly. Dekker grabbed one of Slade's ankles and dragged him to the edge of the bed. Slade laughed as Dekker released his leg and pulled Slade to his feet by his wrists. The last person to pull him out of bed like that was his mother, when he was twelve and refused to get up for the first day of school. Dekker kissed him.

"You're beautiful when you smile," Dekker said and gently pulled Slade into the bathroom behind him. He started the shower, waiting for the water to warm, and enjoyed the soft, lingering kisses Slade peppered across his shoulder blades. He was semi-hard again when he finally stepped beneath the spray, pulling Slade in behind him.

"I'd love to go for another round, but I've got to go in and pay Raven. She's meeting me at two, but I didn't bother tallying up the sales last night, so I need to go in early and do that," Slade said, watching with intense interest as Dekker soaped up.

"I need to go in and do inventory after last night, too. We can meet later and have dinner or something, if you want," Dekker said.

Dekker washed and rinsed his hair and then switched places with Slade. He ran his hands over his face and hair, squeezing the excess water from the shoulder-length strands. Dekker watched Slade just as intently as Slade had watched him. Slade finished washing up quickly and shut the water off.

Half an hour later they were dressed and ready to go. Slade was only slightly smaller than Dekker, so he had borrowed a pair of jeans and a T-shirt that said "Meat Eater." Dekker had winked at him when he'd handed Slade the shirt. Slade laughed and shook his head as he pulled it on.

"Where do you find these damn things?" Slade asked as he followed Dekker out to his truck. They climbed in, and Dekker turned the ignition. Slade ran his hand over the silk-screen on his chest.

"They're gifts from Rex. I think he buys them online," Dekker answered.

"Been friends with him for a long time?" Slade asked. "I watched you at the barbecue. You're close with him, with all of them."

"I met Rex and Logan at the gym almost ten years ago. We hit it off. Our senses of humor meld well. As for the twins, they came later. I'm sure you've noticed the boys are a lot younger than their boyfriends. I honestly don't remember how they hooked up, it just sort of happened. One day they were just...there. You know?"

"What about Alek and Aaron?" Slade asked.

"Aaron and I finished our last year of college together. We majored in business. He was a double major, though. He's a psychologist and does relationship counseling. Does rather well for himself."

"That makes him pairing off with Tony all the more odd," Slade said. "Are they still together?"

"Yes. Joined at the hip, so to speak. We invite them everywhere as a couple now. They look strange together, but on a deeper level they've got a lot in common."

Slade nodded thoughtfully before glancing at Dekker sideways. "And Alek? How did you meet him?"

"He came to the store one day, handing out fliers about volunteer openings at his clinic. It was about the same time the twins were making their moves on Rex and Logan, and I was feeling lonely. I don't remember who asked who out, but we ended up dating for a few months. The relationship never moved to the bedroom, so Alek broke it off. We have mutual friends, so we saw each other all the time, and the friendship never died. About a year later, he asked me to give him a second go, and I said yes. I tried, hard, but it was just more of the same thing, so we mutually decided to end it. We were meant to be friends, not lovers."

Dekker shrugged and pulled the truck to the curb in front of Trendz. Slade's Mercedes remained where it had been parked the night before, seemingly untouched. Slade let out a pent-up breath. He had been concerned George would have returned to the shop after he found out Slade wasn't home last night and vandalized the car. It was a childish move he didn't put George above. He was relieved he'd been wrong. Slade unbuckled his belt and opened the door. Before climbing out, he leaned over and kissed Dekker. The kiss heated immediately, and Slade pulled back before he got swept up in another of Dekker's toe-curling kisses.

"I'd like to see you again later. Call me when you're done for the day?" Slade requested.

"Will do, handsome."

Slade smiled and nodded as he exited the truck. He closed the door and waved. Dekker waited to pull away from the curb until Slade was inside the gallery, which gave Slade a giddy kind of happiness. He'd never felt cherished before, and he liked it. He stared out the main window until Dekker was out of sight and then went into his office to do the accounting from the show. Slade set his cell phone on the desk so he'd hear it when Dekker called. He booted up the computer and opened up the accounting program he used. He retrieved the receipts and cash from last night out of the safe. Slade pushed as many thoughts of Dekker as possible out of his head and focused on getting his accounts in order. Raven would arrive in a couple of hours to collect her earnings, and Slade had only a guesstimate as to how much that would be until he tallied up every penny.

☆☆☆

Dekker was bone tired, but every time he remembered why, his smile broadened. Slade was finally his. Working side by side with the man on last night's show had been both enjoyable and torturous, but Dekker wouldn't have traded it for anything. It had allowed them to see each other in different circumstances and afforded them time to get to know one another better. During the dating show, Slade had told Dekker that he joked around a lot and could be ridiculous at times. He hadn't lied. When things got too stressful or tense or just excruciatingly boring, Slade would say or do something that would break the ice, all while still remaining completely professional. Dekker admired that. There was nothing remotely professional about Dekker's sense of humor. At least in his line of work, dirty jokes and double entendres were acceptable.

Dekker parked the truck in the lot behind the store and got out. He engaged the locks as he made his way to the metal dock door where deliveries were made. Dekker jangled his keys in his hand, unable to keep the smile off his face. The soft rumble of an engine had him turning to see an older-model sedan pull into the lot. The driver got out and headed toward him. It took Dekker a moment to recognize George. The man was seriously disheveled as though he'd slept in his car or spent the night drinking way past his limit. Dekker heaved a sigh and prayed for patience as he waited for George to join him on the dock.

"What can I do for you, George?" Dekker asked.

Now that Slade was his and George was no longer competition, he could be friendly and professional to the man. George apparently didn't feel the same. Dekker could sense the hostility coming off him in waves.

"Did you fuck him? Did you put your hands on my boyfriend?" George yelled and shoved Dekker in the chest.

He allowed the push to move him out of surprise. The men were equally matched in size, but where George had gone soft in the middle, Dekker was all muscle. If George decided to become more physical, Dekker was going to lay him out.

"Slade isn't yours anymore. He kicked your ass to the curb...again.

Deal with it."

Dekker watched George and waited. The man was almost purple in the face with rage. Dekker didn't understand the obsession George had over Slade. He could understand loving Slade, that was damn easy, but if George loved him so much, why did he have another man on the side? It didn't make sense.

"He's only with you because you brainwashed him. Made him think you were some golden boy by pretending to be so fucking perfect and telling lies about me," George spat out.

Dekker stared at the man in surprise. There were simply no words. Dekker wasn't sure what lies he was supposed to have told. George stuck his dick in someone other than Slade. That was a fact, not something Dekker had made up. George misunderstood Dekker's silence and seeming passivity for acquiescence. He got into Dekker's space, practically pressing their chests together. Dekker almost laughed at the man's attempt at intimidation. Obviously, George had an overinflated sense of self.

"Stay the fuck away from my boyfriend, asshole, or I will destroy you." George slowly backed away. He fluttered his hands around his head. "I'll burn it down. Everything you own, gone."

George turned and strutted back to his car. Dekker stood on the dock and watched, stunned. He couldn't believe the audacity of the man, getting in his face, making accusations and threats. What confused him most was what Slade had seen in the man. He was a troll. Once inside, Dekker headed for his office and called Slade about George's little visit. He wanted Slade to be safe and prepared in case George decided to pull the same shit with him. Slade apologized repeatedly about George's behavior, but Dekker kept shrugging it off. It was of no importance. The guy was a narcissistic hothead who was blowing smoke.

Thoughts of Slade and the morning's activities slowly faded behind lists and quantities as Dekker went through what he'd sold the night before and how depleted his stock now was. The distributors he ordered from weren't open on the weekends. He would have to put up "temporarily out of stock" signs if products on the shelves sold out tonight. Dekker had only chosen the stock that would blend well with Raven's artwork, but if any of those IOU's came back today, he'd sell out of those particular items completely. Dekker found it was a problem he was happy to face. The revenue Raven's show had generated would cover the large order he now had to place Monday morning, and he would still be in profit. The few pieces Slade and Raven had hung in the store prior to the show were the perfect addition of tastefully naughty he didn't want to relinquish. They'd taken them down to be displayed at the show, but Dekker made a mental note to discuss buying them with Slade over dinner tonight.

Dekker's phone chimed with an incoming text. It was from Slade and he thumbed open the message.

Called George. Told him we were over and to back off. Think he got the message this time.

Dekker texted back.

Not even a worry. Call you when I'm done here.

Slade sent a smiley face in response. Dekker smiled and refocused on his work. He needed to get this done if he wanted to see Slade anytime soon.

The soft thud of a door closing somewhere in the store jerked Dekker's attention to his closed office door. He glanced at the clock on his computer. It was only two in the afternoon. Callan's Closet didn't open until three on Sundays, and the first of his employees weren't scheduled to show until four. It was the concession Dekker made so the employees could work overnight. He opened and ran the store alone for the first hour until Alexis came in at four. Dixie and Ron would come in at six and work until closing at two a.m. None of his employees should be here this early.

Dekker pushed away from the desk and walked out to the main floor. No one was visible over the shelving and clothing racks. He wandered by the main door and found it still locked, and the digital indicator still functional. If someone had walked through this door, the indicator would have chimed, alerting him. He walked down the hall past his office, through the stockroom to the delivery doors at the back of the building. The garage door was locked down tight. As he approached the heavy metal door that opened to the employee parking lot, he saw that it had been forced open.

He cocked his head. Dekker couldn't recall if he'd reset the alarm after coming in today, but he definitely remembered closing and locking that door. He spun around at the sound of footsteps behind him just as something heavy connected with his temple. Black spots filled his vision, and he dropped to the floor. Dekker pushed himself to his hands and knees, fighting to stay conscious. The battle was lost with another hard hit to the back of his head.

Chapter Thirteen

Slade sat in his apartment, phone in hand, wondering why Dekker hadn't called like he said he would. Slade had worked until six, waiting for Dekker to call and tell him where they were meeting. Assuming Dekker had gotten caught up with his shop, Slade had decided to go home and change into his own clothes. He loved being surrounded by Dekker's scent, but the clothes were a little too big. By eight o'clock, Slade had started to feel like he'd been blown off. He'd dialed Dekker's phone twice, but both calls had gone straight to voicemail. He'd called once an hour after that and was beginning to feel like a stalker. It was almost midnight now, and Slade was finally coming to the conclusion that Dekker wasn't going to call.

"You're not telepathic," Phil said from his seat in the armchair across the room. "Staring at it won't make it ring."

Slade tossed his phone onto the coffee table in irritation and slumped back onto the sofa. He tucked his feet beneath him and folded his arms in childish petulance. Damn it. He thought Dekker was different. The man had been attentive, thoughtful, and respectful, and damn insistent about his attraction to Slade. Slade didn't want to believe that it was all just a ruse to get into his pants, but one date and one business venture together did not mean they knew each other. Depression and hurt set in as Slade's thoughts turned to the connection he'd felt with Dekker, even before they'd had sex this morning. He blamed fatigue for the tears threatening to fall and blew out a sigh. Phil glanced away from the sci-fi movie he was watching and eyed Slade.

"You really do like this guy, don't you?" he asked.

"Pretty fucking sure I'm in love with him or it wouldn't hurt so much that he's ignoring me," Slade admitted. He shook his head. Phil gave a crooked grin that reminded Slade of sympathy. "Fuck it. I'm going to bed," Slade huffed and left the room.

He went through his nightly routine without thinking about it, his mind drifting over every second he'd spent with Dekker, trying to find the moment things had gone wrong. He couldn't find it. He had no idea why Dekker had gone back on his word, and it was making him crazy thinking about all the what-ifs. Would George have gone so far as to slash Dekker's truck tires or paint graffiti on his store walls? Slade didn't believe Dekker would write him off because George turned out to be an asshole, but he wasn't certain. Slade crawled between cold sheets, feeling like he'd been thoroughly played. After hours of tossing and turning, his thoughts circling in his brain without an end in sight, he gave up on sleep.

Trendz and The Cellar were closed on Sundays and Mondays, so sleep wasn't required at the moment. Slade could nap off and on during the day today. He had nothing else to do, especially since Dekker had given him the major brush-off. He'd harbored fantasies all day about how he and Dekker would spend that night and Monday morning wrapped in each other's arms. Now he just felt stupid for even allowing himself to have them. As Slade padded into the living room, he remembered that last kiss and Dekker's promise to call. It had been sincere and genuine. So why hadn't he called?

Slade sat in his usual spot on the sofa and tucked his feet beneath him. Phil had fallen asleep in the recliner, and the DVD he'd been watching earlier played the menu feature repeatedly. Slade picked up the remote and shut the DVD player off. He flicked through stations and infomercials until he found an early-morning news broadcast. He half watched the newsreel while obsessing over Dekker, the sex they'd had, and the lack of communication. No matter how hard he tried, Slade couldn't let it go. The entire situation felt wrong and challenged everything he believed about Dekker and their fledgling relationship.

He watched the ticker across the bottom of the screen letting everyone watching know there were tornadoes and large hail falling east of the city. Slade could hear the distant thunder from the storms. The anchor began a story that had taken place early Sunday afternoon. She told viewers the fire that had destroyed a business on the corner of Reed and Communion was now under investigation as possible arson. Slade's attention turned fully to the story. He knew the intersection, knew the businesses occupying the busy corner, and knew Callan's Closet was among them.

"Phil," Slade yelped as he jumped to his feet. Phil jerked awake and launched the chair into the sitting position.

The news footage from Sunday afternoon showed a reporter standing beside a fire truck. The building behind her was blazing, flames licking at the roofline and black smoke billowing out the windows and doors. Just enough of the sign above the large picture window was visible through the smoke. It wouldn't have mattered if it had been completely destroyed. Slade recognized the building. The signage identifying it as Callan's Closet was only further confirmation that the man he loved had just lost his livelihood.

Several feelings bombarded Slade at once. Relief now that he knew the reason Dekker hadn't called. Regret followed as Slade began to kick himself for being angry over the missed phone call. Both were immediately replaced by dread so cold Slade wrapped his arms around his stomach and shivered. The anchor had returned to the screen and reported that two male victims had been pulled from the burning building by firefighters but one had been pronounced dead at the scene.

Northern General had listed the other victim as critically injured but stable. Slade couldn't stop the tears this time. They slid down his face as the realization that Dekker might have died hours after leaving him settled deep into his heart, ripping it apart. His legs gave out, and he landed hard on the sofa.

"What's happening?" Phil asked. He pushed from the chair and came to sit next to Slade, awkwardly pulling him into a hug.

"Dekker," Slade choked out.

Slade lost all ability to speak as his throat closed up with grief, so he just pointed to the television. Phil looked where he pointed, but it was clear he was still confused. He planted a quick kiss on Slade's temple and rushed out of the room with a muttered "Don't move." Slade couldn't move if he tried. His body was numb. His thoughts were cloudy. Slade lay on his side across the sofa cushions, curled himself into a ball, and cried. The pain had to be released from his body somehow. It would kill him if he kept it inside; Slade was certain of that.

Phil came into the room fully dressed with his phone pressed to his ear. In his other hand he carried clothes and a pair of shoes for Slade. He dropped them on the arm of the sofa and knelt down in front of Slade. He brushed the hair from Slade's forehead and gently massaged his head and neck. Slade didn't respond. It took everything he had to simply breathe. Asking anything more of him right now would be too much, and Phil seemed to understand that.

"Alek, I'm..." Phil said into the phone but stopped, intently listening to whatever it was Alek was telling him. Slade watched his roommate's face turn pale, and Phil closed his eyes. Slade squeezed his eyes shut, and new pain bloomed in his chest. Whatever Phil was being told, it wasn't good. Phil's voice was dimmed by the thumping of his heart in his ears. Slade's mind barely registered that Phil had hung up the phone and was now pulling him to his feet.

It was all a blur until Phil led Slade through the hospital up to the emergency room. Seven of Dekker's friends sat together in one corner of the waiting area. Logan had an arm around Josh. Justin sat on one of Rex's knees. Aaron and Tony sat side by side holding hands. The sight had Slade's grief receding and hope taking up residence. These men wouldn't be here if Dekker was dead. Alek rose and greeted Phil with a hug. The men spoke in hushed tones Slade couldn't hear clearly. His eyes stayed with the men in Dekker's life as they all stood and faced him, their expressions a mixture of sadness and anger. Slade swiped at the tears on his cheeks with his palms and took a deep fortifying breath. Dekker was alive. He had to focus on that. Slade cleared his throat and looked directly at Rex.

"He's okay?" Slade asked quietly.

Everyone shuffled their feet, looked at each other, and acted generally uncomfortable. The response to his question had Slade's concern over losing Dekker rearing its ugly head again. Being alive didn't mean that Dekker would be okay. Maybe he had lost a limb to the fire. Maybe he was brain-dead and would never be more than a vegetable. Fresh tears leaked from Slade's eyes.

"Please?" he begged. "Tell me."

Rex nodded and took Slade by the arm. He led him to the opposite end of the waiting room and gestured to the chair beside him as he took a seat. Slade watched the others take their seats and talk quietly among themselves. Only Justin watched Slade and Rex, his expression unreadable. The sound of Rex's voice pulled Slade's attention off Justin.

"I gotta be honest with you," Rex said, looking Slade in the eye. "I got no idea how to do this."

"Just say it. Please? I know our relationship is still new...just got serious yesterday, but..."

"You and Dek are together now?" Rex asked.

Slade nodded. He was trying hard not to break down in tears again, so speaking wasn't going to happen for a minute. Rex leaned forward, elbows on knees, and ran both hands over his buzzed head.

"Shit, this is bad," Rex muttered. He leaned back in his chair and caught Justin's eye. Rex blew him a kiss, and Justin's lips quirked up into a half smile before quickly slipping back into a grim line. Rex blew out a loud breath.

"Dek is alive, but he's hurt. They have him listed as critical but only because his throat and lungs were injured from smoke inhalation, and he's struggling to breathe. He's got a nasty burn on his left shin that will probably scar, and he has a severe concussion. But, he'll be fine...eventually."

Relief flooded Slade, and he let himself cry. Rex rubbed his back until he was able to control his emotions. He offered the man at his side a watery smile. Rex winked and then looked across the waiting room to his boyfriend. Justin tilted his head to indicate the hallway behind secured double doors that led to the emergency department exam rooms.

"Come on," Rex said and pushed to his feet. He and Slade rejoined the group just as a female cop exited the doors and approached the front desk. Alek pointed at the policewoman.

"That's Sergeant Pratt. You need to go talk to her," Alek said.

"Why?" Slade asked.

Alek was saved from answering when Sergeant Pratt walked over. She was an older woman with graying brown hair pulled into a low ponytail. The lines on her face suggested she was a career cop who'd seen just about everything. She extended her hand to Slade and then Phil.

"I'm Sergeant Melissa Pratt. You're new faces since I arrived."

"Slade Gannon. My roommate and I just got here."

"Phil Lassiter," Phil said as he shook the officer's hand. She nodded

118

at Phil then returned her attention to Slade.

"Mr. Gannon, will you come with me?"

Sergeant Pratt didn't wait for an answer. She took off across the waiting room to a hall that led to the bathrooms. Slade followed, still feeling completely detached from what was going on around him. His brain just couldn't grasp everything that had happened in the past hour. It had been an emotional roller coaster. As he joined Sergeant Pratt in a tiny break room with vending machines and a water fountain, he couldn't shake the feeling this joyride from hell was nowhere near over. Sergeant Pratt pulled out two chairs and took a seat. She pointed to the other and waited for Slade to sit down. She pulled out a pad of paper and a pen. Slade watched and waited, his stomach cramping up in knots.

"First let me tell you that I'm sorry for everything you're going through right now. This conversation won't be easy, I'm afraid."

Sergeant Pratt looked Slade directly in the eye, and Slade nodded. He appreciated her no-nonsense approach. His brain was too preoccupied, his emotions too raw to be deciphering hidden meanings.

"I need you to tell me about your relationship with the victims," she said.

Slade was already confused. He vaguely remembered the news report stating there were two male victims, but it hadn't occurred to him that he would know both. He had yet to learn who the second victim was. "Dekker is my boyfriend...at least I think he is. We just started seeing each other so...I'm not..." Slade swallowed hard then shook his head. "I don't know who the other man was..."

Sergeant Pratt flipped a page in her notebook. "His name was George Westin." She looked up at Slade. "I was told you were in a relationship with him."

Slade couldn't breathe. The news that George was dead was bad enough, but to learn he'd been killed in the same fire Dekker had been

119

injured in was a sucker punch to the gut. He could only imagine why George had gone back to Dekker's store, none of the reasons good. The room started to spin, and Slade was peripherally aware of Sergeant Pratt placing his head between his knees, steadying his body with a firm grip.

"Just breathe," she said softly, and Slade sucked in air. "How well did you know Mr. Westin?" she asked after a few moments. Slade's breathing wasn't great, but it was closer to normal. He still felt lightheaded, so he kept his head down. Sergeant Pratt remained on one knee beside him.

"We dated for a while. We broke up Saturday," Slade answered, barely above a whisper.

"Why?"

"He cheated on me."

Fresh tears slid down Slade's cheeks and fell to the floor. He stared at the dirty tile as memories of his time with George played through his head. Slade loved Dekker, but he had cared about George. If he hadn't, Slade wouldn't have been so hurt when George had strayed. He wouldn't have convinced himself George was worth a second try if he hadn't originally felt something for him. The pain of George's death wasn't as sharp as the pain Slade had suffered when he'd thought Dekker had died, but it was there nonetheless. Slade liked to think he and George could have become friends someday, and he grieved his death.

"How did this happen?" Slade whispered. He was asking the cosmos in general, questioning the way fate had played out. Sergeant Pratt answered.

"We're still trying to figure that out, Mr. Gannon. I can tell you that Mr. Callan was hit on the back of the head at least twice. He has two large cuts, and we found a pipe nearby with blood on it. He was found at the back of the store. Mr. Westin is more of a mystery. He was found in the front of the store severely burned, but had no other injuries. The fire was arson as evidenced by a gasoline can and lighter found at the scene. There was also evidence of forced entry in the loading dock area."

Slade shook his head. Things were going from bad to worse. He was thankful he'd kept his head down because his breathing came faster now, and the room swam around him. He was getting tunnel vision on that one floor tile between his toes. The officer's voice reached his ears through the miasma of fog he was floating in.

"I never thought he'd go through with it," Slade whispered.

"I'm sorry?" Sergeant Pratt said. "*He* who and go through with what?"

Sergeant Pratt's words filtered into Slade's mind slowly. Slade answered, relaying the conversation he'd had with Dekker earlier that afternoon about his confrontation with George. Dekker's reassurances that George would never actually do what he'd threatened seemed ridiculously minimalized now. George had been far more vengeful and angry than either of them could have predicted, and Slade explained all that to the policewoman.

"I just can't believe...the George I knew had never attacked another person. Not even me. He would get in my space, try to physically intimidate me, but he never hit me. Why would he just suddenly attack Dekker?"

"From what you've told me about these men, I suspect Mr. Westin broke in to set the fire, but Mr. Callan surprised him..."

"He knew Dekker was there," Slade said softly. "His truck was parked in the lot. He knew..."

"Perhaps Mr. Westin confronted him again? They fought, Mr. Callan was knocked out, and then Mr. Westin set the fire, except he misjudged and ended up setting himself on fire as well. But we may never know, considering the circumstances," Sergeant Pratt said.

The circumstances being Dekker had most likely been unconscious when George started the fire and couldn't tell the police exactly what happened. Slade wondered. He knew George had a temper and was not above doing something childish, but assault and arson were leagues beyond the vandalism and stalker-type phone calls Slade had expected. Slade swayed in his seat. This entire night had beaten him down, and he wasn't feeling well.

"I need you to lie on the floor," Sergeant Pratt said. She tried to guide Slade to the floor gently, but he was bigger than she was, and he had no control over where his body landed. She pulled a chair over and had him rest his feet on the seat with his knees bent. She went to the entry of the lounge and yelled into the waiting room. "I need a nurse in here."

By the time a nurse knelt beside him, Slade's head was clearing, and he was feeling better. The fog had lifted a little, and he didn't feel about two seconds away from passing out. A cool cloth was pressed to his forehead and another across his throat. He noticed Phil and Alek had come into the lounge with the nurse. They stood off to the side watching with obvious concern. Slade saw the two men were holding hands, but was too immersed in his own turmoil to comment. All Slade wanted to do was rewind to the day before and keep Dekker as far away from Callan's Closet as possible so maybe none of this would have happened.

✰✰✰

Everything hurt. Taking a breath caused burning pain throughout Dekker's chest. The doctor who'd come in a few minutes ago to check on him had said his throat and lungs had sustained burns from the heat of the smoke. He had a concussion from being hit on the head, and his left leg had substantial burns where his pants leg had caught fire. Dekker's head throbbed with even the smallest movements, but his leg was blessedly numb. The doctor had informed him that as the skin healed, he would start to feel pain.

His friends were allowed to visit now, but were limited to two at a time until he was no longer considered in critical condition and confined to intensive care. Dekker was being monitored closely because he had stopped breathing twice, once in the ambulance and again in the emergency room. If he stayed stable through the night, he would be moved to another room. Logan and Josh had been first to visit, followed by Justin and Rex. Now he was waiting for Alek.

Dekker had started out disappointed that Slade hadn't been the first man in his room, but now bounced between anger and hurt because Rex had told him Slade had been in the ER. When he'd asked Rex why Slade left without seeing him, Rex couldn't give an answer. Apparently, Slade and a police officer had a conversation, and Phil had taken a visibly upset Slade home. Dekker was lucky to be alive from what he'd been told. His life's work had literally gone up in flames. All he wanted was to see the man he loved, and it was being denied to him. If he'd had the energy, and a lot less pain, he would have hit something. A gentle knock on the door brought Dekker out of his infuriating thoughts. He looked over to see Alek coming in holding the hand of a man he didn't know. Dekker hadn't known Alek was seeing someone. Alek smiled at him.

"Hey there, Dek. You look pretty good, all things considered," Alek said.

He took Dekker's hand and squeezed. Alek was smiling, but his eyes were glassy with unshed tears. Dekker gave a weak smile in return. His throat hurt too much to talk, partly from the smoke burns and partly from the tube that had been shoved down his throat to help him breathe initially. He squeezed Alek's hand, albeit with very little strength.

"This is Phil," Alek said.

"Slade's roommate?" Dekker whispered.

Phil nodded and Alek kissed the man's hand. "We've been seeing each other for a couple of weeks now," Alek said.

"Go get him," Dekker croaked, holding Phil's gaze. Phil looked at the floor and shuffled his feet, but he didn't move or speak. Dekker wanted the man to leave and bring Slade to him, but he wasn't going.

"Dekker..." Alek started and then stopped and looked up at the ceiling.

"Go get him," Dekker repeated a little louder. Maybe Phil simply hadn't heard him the first time. The increase in volume hurt his throat, and Dekker closed his eyes until the pain subsided.

"Slade needs time to process things, Dek. He passed out when Sergeant Pratt told him what happened," Alek said.

Dekker tore his eyes away from his boyfriend's roommate to look at Alek. He knew all the injuries he had suffered and that his business had all but burned to the ground, but he still had no idea what actually happened. As Dekker was about to ask Alek for details, there was another knock on the door. All three men turned to the entryway as a female police officer entered the room. Rex came into the room behind her.

"Mr. Callan," the woman said. "I'm Sergeant Pratt. I need to ask you a few questions."

"Okay. We're heading out, but I'll be back tomorrow to see how you're doing," Alek said. He leaned down and kissed Dekker on the cheek before following Phil out of the room. As Alek passed Rex on the way out the door, the men shook hands. Rex pulled the chair closer to the bed and sat down. Dekker looked at his friend and raised his eyebrows in question.

"You shouldn't be alone for this. Maybe if Slade hadn't been alone when he heard, he'd have handled things better," Rex told him. That had Dekker concerned, and his gaze whipped back to the police officer.

"Sir, how well do you know George Westin?" Sergeant Pratt asked.

Dekker shook his head. The only George he knew was Slade's ex. He looked to Rex for confirmation that they were talking about the same man. Years of close friendship had Rex understanding the question in Dekker's eyes without him having to voice it.

"Yeah, that George," Rex said softly.

"Didn't. Boyfriend's ex," Dekker whispered.

"Can you think of any reason why Mr. Westin would do something like this?" the officer asked.

"Do what?" Dekker still didn't know what had happened.

"Attack you? Burn your business down?" Sergeant Pratt clarified. Her tone suggested she thought Dekker should already know what had taken place. Dekker creased his forehead and turned his attention once again to Rex.

"What?" Dekker croaked, trying to push himself upright in the bed. Pain flared to life in his body, making him catch his breath and fall back to the bed. Rex was on his feet immediately, leaning over Dekker and rubbing his chest.

"Relax, Dek. I know it's a shock, but try to stay calm. Getting excited won't help you," Rex said.

"What happened? I don't remember anything," Dekker whispered into Rex's ear. Rex looked at Sergeant Pratt.

"He doesn't know what happened. I think you should tell him," Rex said to the woman. The officer quickly relayed the events from the day before.

"Mr. Westin broke into your shop. Preliminary investigation leads us to believe his intentions were to burn it down. We originally thought you surprised him by being there so he hit you over the head, but Mr. Gannon seems convinced Mr. Westin had known you were still inside. He poured gasoline all over the front of the store, but he was messy about it and got it on himself. When he lit the gas on the floor, the gas on his shoes and pants lit as well. He died from the flames before the fire department got there. The fire was just reaching the back of the building where firefighters found you unconscious on the floor. They got to you just in time. Flames were burning through part of your pants leg which is how you got the injury to your shin."

Dekker's brain shut down. He was hearing the words the officer said, but they simply wouldn't compute. Dekker had known George had a temper. He'd witnessed it firsthand the night of Slade's show and again when George had confronted him in the parking lot, but he had no idea the man was unhinged. And now George was dead.

An intense need to see Slade pulsed through Dekker's blood. He had to see him, had to know he was okay, to know he was safe. Alek told him Slade had gone home upset, that he'd passed out when the cops told him what had happened. Dekker tried to push himself up again, but Rex easily held him down with one hand to his chest. Dekker couldn't think beyond his desire to be with Slade. Slade had lost someone close to him, someone he had once cared about, and Dekker needed to be there to help him through the grief. And he needed Slade to help him through the healing process. The cop was suddenly over him, helping Rex keep him down.

"Sir, you need to calm down. Hurting yourself won't help anything."

"Dek, if you don't stop, they're going to sedate you," Rex told him.

"I need him," Dekker said, gripping Rex's wrist. "Please."

Rex kept his hand on Dekker's chest as he pulled his cell phone out of his back pocket with the other. He dialed a number and then put the phone to his ear. Dekker's strength evaporated, and he stopped struggling. He was suddenly very tired. He fought to keep his eyes open as Rex made his call.

"I'll come back tomorrow when you're calmer," Sergeant Pratt said. She left the room quietly. Dekker kept his attention on Rex.

"Hi, it's Rex. Listen, he's not doing too good right now. Talk to him?" Rex paused for a few seconds as whoever it was on the other end of the phone responded. "Okay," he said and then handed the phone to Dekker.

"Hello?" Dekker said into the phone. He had no idea who he was talking to, or if they could even hear him.

"Hi." Slade's warm, husky voice immediately put Dekker at ease.

"I want you here," Dekker said as his eyes watered. He squeezed his lids against the tears.

"I'm sorry. It was just too much and I..." Slade sobbed on the other end of the phone, and it was Dekker's undoing. A tear rolled down his cheek. "God, Dekker, I'm so sorry. I'm sorry this happened. I'm sorry I'm not handling it well, and that I...can't...be there for you. I'm in a fog, can't think straight. Pretty sure this is what insanity feels like."

"Slade," Dekker whispered. Damn, his throat and chest were hurting something fierce. "Not your fault," he said despite the pain talking elicited. "Come." Slade's response was not what he wanted to hear.

"I need some time, Dekker. You're hurt and you lost the store. You already have a lot to deal with. You don't need me and my shit, too. I'm so overly emotional. The doctor who checked me out called it shock, and George wouldn't have done this if it weren't for me. I just...I need to be alone for a while, to process."

It felt too much like good-bye for Dekker, and the dam burst, tears falling freely. He needed Slade with him so badly, and Slade wasn't coming. A pain that had nothing to do with his injuries blossomed in his chest.

"Need you. Love you," Dekker said and heard a muffled "Shit" from Slade.

"This is not how I wanted to do this, but I think I love you, too. Rex promised me that he or one of the others would always be with you. I just...I need a little time. I'm sorry." Slade took a deep shuddering breath. "I have to go."

"No," Dekker whispered through his own tears.

"I do have feelings for you, please remember that," Slade said and then disconnected the call.

Every ounce of strength drained from Dekker's body with that final click. The phone dropped from his hand to the bed as his arm went slack. It was only then he noticed Sergeant Pratt standing in the doorway, and a nurse putting medication into his IV. Rex rubbed Dekker's chest and forehead. The sensation was soothing and, along with the physical injuries, emotional overload, and medication, Dekker was lulled to sleep.

Chapter Fourteen

George's funeral had been unpleasant. Slade had come face to face with George's very distraught boyfriend, Rowan, who didn't want Slade there. Rowan had been quite vocal about it, too. To Slade's surprise, Rowan had known who he was the moment he set foot in the funeral home, and he had no idea how that was possible. Slade had only ever heard Rowan's voice over the phone. He'd learned about George's side action the first time when George was in the shower one night, and a text had come through on his phone. *Bed is cold without you. Will you be here soon?*

Slade had broken up with him before he'd even finished his shower, yelling at him while he dried off and deflecting every excuse given as George dressed. After the funeral, he'd learned that George had met both him and Rowan about the same time and had been dating them simultaneously. According to Rowan, it was Slade's fault George was dead. Logically, he knew Rowan's argument was ridiculous, and someday when the grief wasn't as strong, Rowan would see that, too. Slade wished his emotions were as logical as his brain. He knew he wasn't responsible for George's actions, but he *felt* responsible. And the guilt was eating him alive.

That morning he had warred with himself about even going to the damn funeral until Phil made the decision for him. Once there, Slade admitted that he needed to say good-bye, to close that chapter once and for all. Now four weeks later, Slade still fought the crippling depression that had gripped him since the fire. The world carried on normally. His businesses continued to do well, but Slade went day to day in a fog. Something was broken inside him, and he couldn't figure out how to fix it.

Phil had convinced him to take a trip to the department store with him today. According to Phil, Slade was becoming difficult to live with, and he'd had enough. Sitting in the passenger seat of Phil's Volvo on the way home after a morning of shopping, Slade felt like shit. Every corner brought back one memory or another of George or Dekker. Slade became obsessed with thoughts of George and the fact that he had attacked Dekker and destroyed his livelihood.

"I betrayed him," Slade said, thinking of Dekker. Slade stared out the side window but wasn't really seeing anything. Phil sighed heavily. Slade knew he was beginning to sound like a broken record.

"No, you didn't," Phil said. "But you do need to go see him."

"How am I supposed to face him? After what George did...it's my fault. If I hadn't told him to go fuck himself, he wouldn't have gone after Dekker. Why would he even want to see me?"

"Because he loves you. Alek tells me he's driving the twins nuts. They're apparently little gossipers, and Dekker has decided they should know everything about what's going on with you, which then leads them to complain to Logan and Rex, who then call me because you won't answer the phone. Even Aaron has called me, and I've only met him once," Phil said as he maneuvered the car down a crowded residential street. Slade looked down and twisted his hands together in his lap.

"Do you love him?" Phil asked as he slowed the car down.

"Yes," Slade answered. He looked up when he realized Phil was pulling into a driveway. A quick look around his surroundings revealed Phil had driven them to Rex's house.

"Good. Now, get in that house."

"Why are we here?" Slade asked.

A knot grew in his gut as he got out of the car. He could hear the voices and laughter coming from the backyard. Flashbacks of the first time he'd come here popped into his head. That day had been the beginning of the end for his relationship with George.

"Celebratory cookout. Dekker got the insurance settlement yesterday, and he's rebuilding his business. He wanted you here, and you need to be here. You need to see him."

"I can't go in there," Slade said. Phil was already halfway up the walk when he turned around. "I'm the reason he was attacked, and then I hurt him even more by ignoring him. How can I possibly face him after that? I'm a horrible person," Slade said in response to Phil's angry expression.

Phil blew out a breath and practically stomped back to stand in front of Slade. He leaned in close. "No, you're not. George's attack had nothing to do with you. That's on him. The fucker went nuts. God only knows why. And like I said, I've talked to Logan and Rex a lot. I mentioned you were depressed and not acting normal. No doubt they've told Dekker. No one, and I mean no one, in that house blames you for anything. Let's go."

Phil grabbed Slade's arm and pulled him toward the house. Slade felt like he was being dragged through sludge born of self-hate and fear. He allowed Phil to lead him into the house because what choice did he have? Phil had driven, which gave Slade no easy exit. Phil released his arm in the living room and continued out into the backyard. Slade stood there for a moment. He hadn't seen Dekker since the day of the fire; he hadn't visited him in the hospital, and he hadn't spoken to Dekker since the phone call when he'd told him he loved him. An overwhelming need and desperate hope that Phil might be right that no one blamed him, that *Dekker* didn't blame him, propelled Slade out the sliding glass door onto the deck.

Dekker was reclining on a chaise lounge with his legs outstretched, his injured leg propped up on a pillow. The man looked as gorgeous as ever. Conversation stopped, and all eyes were on Slade as he stepped onto the deck. When Dekker turned his head to see what everyone was staring at, Slade was instantly lost in those hazel eyes. Dekker's features went from sad to surprised to full-on joyful in a heartbeat. Dekker was on his feet in seconds, and Slade met him halfway. Dekker wrapped his arms around Slade's waist and crushed him to his chest.

Slade immediately knew he'd handled things wrong. He should have glued himself to Dekker's side and allowed them to heal each other. It wasn't a mistake he would make again. The moment Slade opened his mouth to say just that, Dekker kissed every thought from his mind. And just like that, everything was put right in Slade's universe.

Chapter Fifteen

The past month melted away. The pain, the doubt, the fear, all of it ceased to matter now that Slade was back in his arms. Dekker held him tightly against his body as he plundered Slade's mouth. He still didn't understand why Slade had kept his distance. Phil had bounced the term depression around, but it didn't matter right now. Lips sealed tightly on Dekker's, Slade adjusted his body until the fit was perfect. He fisted Dekker's hair and rolled his hips, grinding his erection against Dekker's pelvis. Dekker grabbed Slade's ass and pulled the man hard against him, bucking his hips, rubbing their rapidly hardening cocks together. One of Dekker's friends cleared his throat, reminding Dekker and Slade they weren't alone. Slade broke the kiss, but kept his body pressed firmly against Dekker.

"I'm sorry," Slade said.

Even if Slade had wanted to move away from Dekker, it would never happen. Dekker had serious strength, and his grip on Slade was iron tight. Slade relaxed his body and Dekker eased his grip slightly. Slade rested his cheek against Dekker's shoulder in silent communication that he wasn't leaving, and Dekker's desperate hold turned into a loving embrace.

Dekker breathed deeply; relief that he hadn't lost Slade to this whole disaster pushed him to the verge of tears. His friends had done their best to keep him from going out of his mind and had managed to keep him this side of sane. The moment he had allowed Alek to talk him into a night of exhibition and humiliation almost three months ago had been the beginning of his downfall. Dekker would forever be grateful for Alek's insistence he take part because it had brought Slade into his life. Dekker knew he'd fallen in love with Slade at the first sound of his voice. The blind date and everything that followed was simply formality, all of it leading to this moment. Dekker swallowed the lump forming in his throat as Slade nuzzled into the hollow behind his ear.

"I love you," Dekker whispered.

Slade kissed the skin just below Dekker's ear before whispering, "I think I love you, too."

Dekker turned his head until their lips were brushing against one another, fanning the embers that had been smoldering below the surface into full-fledged flames.

"Next time, we do this together. You don't get to hide away like that again."

"Okay," Slade agreed.

"Marry me," Dekker said.

Slade pulled back and stared into Dekker's eyes. Dekker would have given his right leg, which still felt oddly numb at the burn site, to know what Slade was thinking in that moment. He hadn't meant to propose quite like this, or at this exact moment, but the words were out of his mouth before his brain knew what was happening. Slade's eyes glistened with unshed tears, and he smiled. He was taking too long to answer, and Dekker couldn't really blame him. The proposal had come out of the blue and surprised both of them.

"You don't have to answer right now, but at least you know what I'm aiming for. And I'll ask you again." Then in his best Bogart impersonation he said, "I will be your husband, Slade; maybe not today, maybe not tomorrow, but soon and for the rest of your life."

Dekker's proclamation was met with laughter from Slade and groans and boos over his horrible acting skills from everyone else. He kissed Slade's forehead before tugging him over to the lounge chair. Dekker sat as far to one side as he could. He pulled Slade down beside him and smiled when Slade curled against him, resting his head on Dekker's chest.

"Have you ever been to Vegas?" Slade asked once they were comfortable.

"No, but I hear they have strippers," Dekker answered.

"Oh, for the love of God," Alek mumbled.

Epilogue

Eight Months Later

Dekker sat in his office, finalizing all the details before his grand reopening tomorrow. Finding a new space for his shop had been surprisingly easy, and with the help of his friends, it was fully stocked and ready to go in record time. He was extremely pleased with the new location for the simple fact it was close to Slade. Slade had helped him negotiate a deal on an empty space down the street from Trendz and The Cellar.

Dekker loved being within walking distance of his man. It gave them more time to spend together. They drove together every day, and if time allowed, they would meet for lunch. Slade was moving in with Dekker in stages, giving Phil time to find a new roommate. There was currently a bet going on whether or not that new roommate would be Alek. Dekker was out fifty dollars if Alek did move in with Phil. He didn't believe Alek and Phil were all that serious about each other. Dekker just didn't see the spark between them that he saw between Rex and Justin, or Josh and Logan, or the fireworks that existed between him and Slade.

Dekker's phone buzzed with an incoming text. He lifted it to see a message from Slade. *Special delivery for you at the back door. Let him in.* Dekker pocketed his phone and went to the delivery door at the back of his store. His heart took on a nervous flutter as he walked through the stockroom. Since the fire, he was edgy when in the backroom alone, but he pushed through the anxiety every time, and it lessened a bit each day.

He opened the door to find Logan leaning against the brick wall across the alley.

"Hi," Dekker said in surprise. He stepped back to let his friend enter.

"Are you busy?" Logan asked as he passed.

Dekker closed and locked the door before giving Logan his full and completely confused attention. "No. Why?"

Logan faced him and smiled broadly. He clapped his hands and then rubbed his palms together quickly. The action made him look maniacal. Now Dekker was not only confused, but concerned.

"Slade is sending you on a surprise scavenger hunt, and I'm here to get you started," Logan answered.

"Really? That sounds...cool," Dekker said as a smile slowly crept across his face. "Let me shut down the computer, and I'll be ready to go."

Dekker walked back to his office with Logan following. He closed the document he'd been looking over. As the computer logged off and shut down, Dekker gathered his things off the desk. Logan waited at the door with his hands in the pockets of his jeans.

"I'm happy for you, Dek," Logan said. "You're such a unique and wonderful man. I'm glad you finally found someone worthy of you. You're a little impulsive and crazy at times, but Slade doesn't seem to mind."

"Nah. It's why he loves me. I make his life exciting," Dekker said.

He draped an arm over Logan's shoulders and led him out the front door of the store where his truck was parked on the street. Logan's sleek Corvette was parked behind it. Dekker looked down the street toward Trendz. He had dropped Slade off there this morning.

"If I do this scavenger hunt, how will Slade get home?" Dekker asked.

"Me. I'm taking him home as soon as I see you off," Logan said. He pulled a slip of paper wrapped around a wad of cash from his back pocket. "Josh is being held hostage at Town Crossings Mall by a haberdasher demanding seven hundred thirty-six dollars in ransom. Find him and rescue him," Logan read and handed the cash to Dekker.

Dekker laughed. "Haberdasher?"

"Yeah. Your boyfriend's as odd as you. Anyway, get going. You have four more clues after this."

Thirty minutes later, Dekker was thankful he knew what a haberdasher was. He'd been able to narrow down his search for Josh to the clothing stores that catered only to men. He found Josh and Phil lounging in chairs near the changing rooms. Josh smiled and leapt to his feet as Dekker approached. Dekker smiled back and handed Josh the seven hundred thirty-six dollars in cash Logan had given him.

"Your ransom, good sir."

"Thanks," Josh said and pushed open the nearest changing room door.

"Put the suit on and then come out, and I'll see what changes need to be made," Phil said.

"You work here?" Dekker asked Phil.

"Yes. Get in there," he answered. Phil smiled and gave Dekker a gentle nudge.

"Okay," Dekker said.

On the drive over and during the subsequent search for Josh, Dekker had decided to go with the flow and not try to understand anything that happened during Slade's scavenger hunt. If it had been him setting up this little game, he would have made it all mysterious only to make sense when the last clue was revealed, and he suspected Slade had done the same. After Phil had made adjustments to the fit of the suit, which looked damn good on him, Dekker changed back into his own clothes and joined Josh outside the store.

"Ready for the next clue?" Josh asked as he fiddled with his little slip of paper.

"Lay it on me," Dekker said.

"Justin has become lost in a jungle of beauty supplies and is being stalked by a cosmetician. Find him and lead him to safety," Josh read.

"A beauty shop in the mall, are you kidding me? There are dozens of those here," Dekker said.

"Happy hunting," Josh said.

He gave Dekker a quick peck on the lips and then walked away. Dekker shook his head. He found a mall directory and located the closest salon to his position. Slade had sent him to an upscale men's clothing store, so he decided to look for Justin in the fancier salons first. Dekker found him at the other end of the mall in the fourth shop he searched. Justin was sitting in a salon chair having a conversation with a female stylist. When Justin saw him, he got up and motioned for Dekker to sit.

"Hi, Lena, nice to see you again," Dekker said as he sat in the chair. Lena and Slade had been best friends since college. Dekker had met her a few times at Slade's art shows.

"She's just going to treat you to a deep conditioning and trim. Okay?" Justin said.

Dekker looked at his hair in the mirror. It was definitely getting long and looked a bit dull. As he thought about it, he realized it had been over a year since he'd last cut it. "Sure, go for it," he said to Lena's reflection.

Lena smiled at him and got to work. An hour later, Dekker and Justin left the salon. Justin headed for the food court. He hadn't given Dekker his next clue yet, so Dekker followed. Dekker saw Josh and Logan at a table sharing nachos. He stared at the couple as Justin stopped and faced him. He was suddenly very curious how Slade had managed to time everything so perfectly, especially considering there was no telling how long it would take Dekker to find each of his friends.

"How are you guys managing this?" Dekker asked.

"Texting and a willingness to wait," Justin answered. "As Lena was finishing up with you I texted everyone. Josh texted me while you were changing." Justin shrugged and unfolded his paper so he could read Dekker's next clue. Logan and Josh saw them and waved. Dekker smiled back at them and listened to Justin.

"Rex has become overwhelmed by an overzealous bartender listing the varieties of grapes at your favorite vineyard. Help him order the best."

"Shit," Dekker said and covered his eyes with his hands. "I don't remember Slade's favorite wine."

"What makes you think it has to be Slade's favorite? Why can't it be yours? He just said the best," Justin said.

Dekker blew out a breath and dropped his hands. He dug around in his pocket for his keys. "Yeah, okay."

He hugged Justin and waved at Logan and Josh as he headed for the exit. The entire drive over to The Cellar, which was by far his favorite vineyard, he wracked his brain trying to remember Slade's favorite wine and simply couldn't. Dekker parked his truck behind Rex's Jeep and yanked his phone out. He typed The Cellar into Google. The website loaded and he pulled up the wine list. He read down the list and quickly became overwhelmed himself. This was the most difficult clue so far. Dekker knew nothing about wine. He gave up with a sigh and went inside to join Rex at the bar.

"What were you doing out there?" Rex asked as Dekker sat down on the barstool beside him.

"Trying to figure out which wine is the best," Dekker answered.

Rex chuckled. "Slade said you'd have a hard time with this one."

Dekker waited to see if Rex would throw him a bone, give him some idea what he was supposed to order, but the man just sat there smiling at him. Slade's bartender, Jose, came out of the back office and leaned his elbows on the bar. He smiled at Dekker.

"Good evening. What can I get you?" Jose asked with a sparkle in his eyes. Slade really had gone all out for this little hunt. At each location, Dekker found one of his friends accompanied by one of Slade's friends. It warmed Dekker's heart to know they had such support and acceptance around them. He propped his chin in his hand and sighed.

"Um...a bottle of your best wine?" Dekker asked shyly.

Rex and Jose both laughed. "Nicely played," Jose said and Rex clapped Dekker on the back. "Don't tell Slade I let you off the hook so easily, though," Jose added as he pulled a bottle of wine from under the bar and set it down in front of Dekker.

Dekker spun the bottle around so he could read the label. "Is this Slade's favorite wine?" he asked.

"No, but it pairs well with the spices used in Tibetan food," Jose answered.

Dekker didn't know what to say. Emotions bubbled up inside him. He had no idea what the suit, haircut, and wine meant, but the thought and care Slade had put into every stop showed Dekker just how much Slade loved him. Rex yanked Dekker against him with a strong arm around the shoulders and planted a kiss to his temple.

"No crying. You have one more clue," Rex said softly.

"I'm not crying," Dekker said. "Yet."

Rex released Dekker and pulled the clue from beneath his wine glass. "The man responsible for everything is buried beneath a mound of forms at the fundraiser's benefactor. Help dig him out," he read.

Dekker took the wine and said good-bye to Rex and Jose. Suit, haircut, and wine, and now he was heading to the clinic to find Alek. The scavenger hunt was fun and Dekker was enjoying every second of it, but he had absolutely no idea what Slade's endgame was. Despite his original resolution of just going with the flow, Dekker had still spent every second trying to figure out where all this was leading. He was still trying to figure it out when he parked beside Alek's Honda. There was another car in the lot that he didn't recognize, but if Slade kept true to form, the owner of the vehicle would be one of Slade's friends.

Normally at this time of night the clinic would be closed, but he found the front door open. He walked into the lobby and found Alek sitting on one of the sofas, talking to Rowan. Dekker was both shocked and pleased to find Rowan taking part. George had been dating both Slade and Rowan at the same time. They hadn't known about each other at first and had met for the first time at George's funeral. According to Slade, the meeting hadn't gone well, but a few months later, Rowan had contacted Slade and asked to meet. They had bonded over mutual betrayal and memories and become good friends.

The men rose to their feet, and Dekker wrapped Alek in a tight hug. Dekker whispered his thanks in Alek's ear, and Alek responded with a whispered "You're welcome." If it hadn't been for Alek insisting Dekker take part in the dating show, he would never have met Slade, and he would be forever grateful to Alek for that. Dekker then turned to Rowan and yanked him into a hug. In an odd twist of fate, Rowan was responsible for Slade and Dekker being together, too. After all, it had been Rowan's voice Slade had overheard during that fateful phone call with George that had finally pushed Slade into Dekker's arms.

Dekker hoped that tonight would help Rowan relax around him. They had a strained coexistence because of George's attack on Dekker. Dekker didn't blame Rowan any more than he blamed Slade, but both men carried guilt over it for some reason. Alek picked up a thick manila envelope, sealed with packing tape, from the chair behind him. "Do not open" was written across it in bold black lettering. Alek handed it to him, and Dekker raised his eyebrows.

"What am I supposed to do with it if I can't open it?" Dekker asked.

"Take it home. Slade will tell you what to do next," Alek answered.

Dekker looked at Rowan, hoping the younger man would help, but he just smiled apologetically and shrugged in an I-have-no-say kind of way. Dekker was kind of feeling let down. If Alek had been the last stop, shouldn't there have been a big finale? The final reveal that would make everything he'd just done make sense? Dekker stood there with the weight of the envelope in his hands and stared out the window. He shook his head in confusion and disappointment. Rowan touched his forearm tentatively, like he was still unsure if his touch was welcome.

"Go home, Dekker. Slade is waiting for you," Rowan said.

"Take the wine and the envelope inside with you, too," Alek added.

Dekker did as he was instructed. He drove home, occasionally peeking at the bottle of wine in the cup holder and the envelope lying on the passenger seat. He ran all the clues over and over again in his mind and couldn't make sense of them. Dekker was anxious to get home so Slade could connect the dots for him. He couldn't stop thinking about it, trying to puzzle it out, and his head was starting to hurt. And, Dekker realized as he was pulling into the driveway beside Slade's little sports car, he was hungry. As soon as he got the answers from Slade, he was ordering pizza.

Dekker opened the door to the house and was immediately overcome with the heavenly scent of food. Slade stood in the middle of the living room in a pair of boxer shorts and one of Dekker's T-shirts that said "Blessed" with an arrow pointing down. Even dressed for bed the way he was, he looked beautiful. Slade bit his lower lip in a show of nerves. Food containers from House of Nepal sat on the coffee table with two plates and two wine glasses. Dekker held up the wine and envelope with a smile. He had just walked into his big reveal. Slade smiled and took the wine.

"Did you have fun?" he asked.

"Yes, thank you," Dekker said. He hoped Slade could hear the sincerity in his voice.

Slade looked at him through his lashes, a glint in his eyes. "Did you figure it out? What all this is leading up to?"

Dekker shook his head and waved the envelope. "I'm assuming the answer is in here," he said.

"Sit down. I'll be right back," Slade said and disappeared into the kitchen.

Dekker did as instructed. The scent of food made his mouth water, but his curiosity over Slade's plans had him waiting patiently. Slade came back into the living room with the now-open bottle of wine and poured some into each glass. He set the bottle down on the table and picked up a rectangular box wrapped in paper, resembling a road map. He sat down beside Dekker, pressed his body as close as possible, and handed Dekker the gift. As Dekker began unwrapping the box, he noticed the city centered in the middle of it—Las Vegas.

"Is this a map of Nevada?" he asked.

"Yes," Slade answered.

Dekker smiled at the short, uninformative answer. He felt Slade's body tense when he flipped open the lid of the jewelry box. Inside, set on a soft bed of velvet, were two identical silver bracelets engraved with "Forever Yours." Dekker sat frozen. He didn't know what to say or do. He stared at Slade's gift.

"Turn them over," Slade said softly and Dekker did. On the other side of one bracelet was Slade's name and on the other side of the second was Dekker's name.

"They're beautiful," Dekker choked out around unshed tears. He ran his index finger across the engraving of Slade's name. "I wear this one?" he asked.

"Yes, and I wear the one with your name on it. They're engagement bracelets," Slade said. Dekker whipped his eyes to Slade. Dekker had proposed to Slade in the heat of the moment eight months ago, but Slade had never said yes.

"Do you still want to marry me?" Slade asked.

"Hell, yes," Dekker said and kissed Slade hard, slipping his tongue in for a taste when Slade's lips parted. He pushed Slade onto his back and settled on top of him, the food and clues all but forgotten. When Dekker finally let them come up for air, Slade cupped Dekker's face in his hands.

"I analyze and plan everything," Slade said. "But you, you're so impulsive." Slade closed his eyes and pulled Dekker's head down for another soft brush of lips. "God, I hope this is okay," Slade whispered.

"Everything's perfect," Dekker said and rubbed their noses together.

Slade opened his eyes. "Open the envelope."

Dekker lifted off Slade and grabbed the envelope off the corner of the table where he'd put it when he sat down. He tore open the end and pulled out an overstuffed folder with the "Welcome to Las Vegas" sign on the front. What he found inside the folder took his breath away. Plane tickets, hotel reservations, and a wedding announcement. He didn't read any of it. He didn't need to. Slade was telling him what it all meant.

"We fly out next Friday. The wedding is scheduled for two p.m. Saturday. Phil said it would only take a day or two for your suit to be ready. I delivered the invitations in person so I could keep everything quiet. Everyone already has their plane tickets..."

"How long have you been planning this?" Dekker asked, interrupting.

"Since about ten seconds after you asked me to marry you," Slade answered with a smile.

Dekker set the folder aside and picked up the box with the bracelets in it. He ran his fingers lovingly over the engraved names. "What would you have done tonight if I'd said no; not that there was any chance in hell of that, but what if?"

"That thought never crossed my mind," Slade admitted. He pulled the bracelet with his name on it out of the box and secured it around Dekker's left wrist. He then pulled out the bracelet with Dekker's name on it and held it out to Dekker.

"Marry me?" Slade asked. "Next week...in Vegas," he added with a smirk.

Dekker took the bracelet and put it on Slade's left wrist. He kissed one corner of Slade's mouth. "Fuck." A kiss to the other corner. "Yes."

Dekker slipped his tongue into his fiancé's mouth while Slade laughed and wrapped his arms around Dekker's neck. Dekker removed Slade's clothing slowly, worshiped every inch of his body with his lips and tongue, and then made love to him on the couch. When they were done, they reheated the food in the microwave and ate it straight out of the cartons while sitting on the floor naked. They toasted their upcoming nuptials with the entire bottle of wine and fell asleep wrapped around each other on the sofa.

Around one in the morning they woke and moved to the bedroom, where Dekker pushed Slade facedown onto the mattress. Dekker straddled him and massaged Slade's back and shoulders as he pushed deep into Slade's ass. Slade bucked and moaned beneath him, and within a few short minutes, Dekker was yelling his name as he emptied himself. He flipped Slade onto his back and brought him to orgasm with his mouth, sucking until Slade's warm seed covered his tongue. Dekker kissed and licked his way back up his lover's body before settling beside him, cradling Slade in his arms.

"It's going to be a long damn week," Dekker muttered into the darkness.

Slade's soft laughter was the only response.

About the Author

Kay lives in Colorado with her husband and their animal children. Family is important to her, so there are weekly visits to her parents and frequent text messages with her brothers. She has a severe addiction to coffee and Mexican food.

Kay loves to read and write and can easily become consumed by it for hours, much to the dismay of the husband and dogs. On occasion she can even be convinced to venture out into world of the living.

Email: kaydohertyauthor@gmail.com
Twitter: @kdohertyauthor
Pinterest: @KDohertyAuthor

NineStar Press, LLC

www.ninestarpress.com

www.ingramcontent.com/pod-product-compliance
Lightning Source LLC
Chambersburg PA
CBHW020340260626
47156CB00004B/1620